sù fi

CW00797293

ANTANAS MARCELIONIS

MASTER
VERSION 1.1

A near-future sci-fi techno thriller

© Antanas Marcelionis, 2024

First Edition: December 2024

Written and published by Antanas Marcelionis.

Cover artwork and illustrations created by Antanas Marcelionis with the help of Midjourney.

Translated by Martynas Majeris.

Edited by Brendan Harding.

ISBN 978-609-08-0671-5

ANTANAS MARCELIONIS

MASTER

VERSION 1.1

www.masterversion.net

[PREFACE]

Let's start with the most important thing: explaining the premise of how this book came to be. Master Version 1.1 was written by a Lithuanian author at the time when russia's full-scale invasion of Ukraine was rolling into its third year. This war left the whole world shell-shocked, but in our neck of the woods—Eastern and Northern Europe—it imparted the heaviest emotional toll. Footage from bombed cities in Ukraine, reports on the number of people killed and injured, meeting and interacting with refugees who had to drop everything to escape the horrors of the invasion, has long become our daily routine. From our point of view, there are no "sides"—only the aggressor and its target.

For someone who's not as involved in this war as us here, this book might seem one-sided, even permeated with "excessive" contempt towards russia. It is done on purpose to convey the general sentiment of our region.

This brings us to a second thing that might jump out at the reader: russia, russian, putin are not capitalized. It's not something that was invented by the author, but is rather a universal way of expressing passive anger and disdain toward the aggressor and its leader. This tiny token of defiance is used in our daily lives, even in semi-official communications. Replacing this custom with grammatically-correct capitalized terms would've been inconsistent and damaging to the authenticity of the book's mood.

Finally, the nuanced use of the word "russian" deserves a separate explanation. "A russian" means "someone who lives in russia (and is therefore a cog in the aggressor's machine)". It in no way relates to members of russian-speaking communities across the world. We'd never say "a russian" to define a person from London, Kyiv, or Vilnius, for example.

Beeeeeeeep, beep, beep, beep.

A long signal and three short ones—broadcast directly into the nerves in my ear by an implant—jerk me out of a deep sleep. In situations like this, I'd sometimes ask myself: where am I, or who am I? Not this time. In sync with the first signal, the drug delivery module administers a dose of modafinil. I'm fully awake by the time the last beep fades. They say the effect is similar to cocaine, just with a tad less euphoria.

I know I'm on the third floor of a crumbling five-story building. All structures in the gray zone are either already collapsed or in the process of collapsing. Some are literally falling apart as we speak—set off by something as minor as a gust of wind or a loud sneeze (true story).

I'm lying on a moldy mattress in what seems to have once been an angsty teenage girl's room. It looks like she tried to bury her rosy childhood beneath posters of EMO bands I've never heard of. Five youths, decked out in hussar uniforms, glare down at me disapprovingly from a *My Chemical Romance* poster. Riiiight, who are you to judge?

My drones, currently on watch duty on the roof, have identified threats. Three beeps—three potentially dangerous intruders. I slide down the visor of my helmet. Part of my view is now taken up with a video feed from the surveillance copter[1] Magpie.

Having detected a threat, Magpie ascended to an altitude of a hundred meters , aimed its camera at the interlopers, and began tracking them. The drone's propellers make so little noise that it's virtually undetectable from the ground.

Three figures are creeping through the territory of a kindergarten, adjacent to the yard of my building. I switch to thermal vision. Based on their heat signature, they're obvious gavriks[2]—low-level,

---

1   Four-propeller drone.
2   Russian slang for "pal" or "buddy", used in a belittling way.

unregistered trespassers. The first one isn't wearing a helmet (Barehead), the second is grossly overweight (Fatty), and the thuggish demeanor of the last one clearly identifies him as the group's leader (Top Dog).

An encounter with such a low-level enemy may not qualify as premium content, but it's better than nothing.

[Start live]

Master—a name Ukrainians bestowed upon me years ago—pops up in the Warvid.Zone live streamer list. Nearly half a million followers receive a notification: it's on!

My guests are loitering behind a white brick wall of what used to be a gazebo. The rock dust slates that served as its roof have long been shattered to pieces. I wish my new friends would get cancer from all the asbestos, but somehow, I doubt they'll last that long.

Magpie's video feed makes it perfectly clear: there's a quarrel underway.

The dudes stop the arm-waving and start shaking their hands: rock-paper-scissors, or more like their russian equivalent—"vas ki chi," although they're probably calling out "po morskomu"[1]! Top Dog, in validation of his superiority, claims the first win and steps away. Fatty and Barehead go at it again. The latter, grossly annoyed, kicks the wall of the gazebo. The kick is successful: a loose brick comes off and lands nearby.

"Got owned, huh?"

The loser angrily pulls a bottle-sized object from his backpack and stashes it in a concealed pocket of his jacket, a space that was probably intended for bottle storage by design. He accepts a helmet from Top Dog—it curiously resembles one from WW2— tinkers with the attached camera, and puts it on. Fuck, how am I supposed to call him now?

[Scan video signal frequencies]

[Signal found]

[Decoding]

....

1   Sailor style.

8

A POV[1] video feed from Barehead (nah, I'm not changing his nickname) pops on my visor. I listen in on their comms:

"Don't piss yourself, Ginger (fine, I can use two names)—there's nobody there."

"Go fuck yourself, Lard." (I almost got it right)

"Beat it already."

"Yeah yeah, going."

Barehead, a.k.a.[2] Ginger, pokes half a head out from the gazebo and looks around. He covers a few meters to the kindergarten's fence, then clumsily rolls over the top. Breathing heavily, he trots to the nearest stairwell of the building I'm in; mine is the one furthest away.

Should I wait for my guest to arrive? Probably not—my stream's spectators aren't *that* patient.

I grab my Daniel Defense rifle. Hunching to avoid being visible through the windows, I run to the end of the hallway. I exit to the stairwell, and descend while watching Ginger enter the first apartment and check its rooms one-by-one.

I stop at the bottom, just near the exit.

My larger drone, Crow, is up in the air with Magpie, but just a bit higher—analyzing the area at a wider angle. I'm not watching Crow's video—there's no need for that yet.

[Video feed on]

Three barely transparent windows obscure the real view—a disgusting, snot-covered green wall in front of me. Someone armed with sharp objects and markers has left a treasure trove of information on it: *Толик—пидор*[3] or *Я* ♥ *Лену*[4]. I might get to that later.

....

1   Point of view.

2   Also known as.

3   Tolik is a fag.

4   I love Lena.

I sit tight for a half-minute.

"Ground floor—empty. Going up."

Reports Ginger.

"Move your ass."

Top Dog urges him on.

Showtime!

[Manual mode]

I guide Crow a bit further behind the enemies and make it drop to just a few meters. The prime subjects of my attention are now directly in its crosshairs. I urge the drone toward them.

From this close, the gavriks finally hear the sounds coming from the approaching Crow (hint: it's not "caw") and begin to turn toward it.

[Fire]

A heavy metallic dart is launched from the drone by an electromagnetic impulse. It covers the distance to Top Dog's head in a fraction of a second, punctures his lobe, and lodges itself in the back of his skull.

For a moment, he wears a perplexed look that says *What the fuck was that?!*, then hits the ground and establishes a direct connection with whatever gods he used to pray to.

Right after the shot, I make the drone lurch upward, perform a loop, and then hang in place. Fatty is now on the run. Unfortunately for him, as he tries to steal a glance back, he trips over the brick Ginger dislodged earlier and nosedives into the mud. His huge ass is a perfect target—no body armor down there.

[Fire]

A dart in the soft tissue of an ass isn't what you would consider a serious injury, but the poison it's tipped with paralyzes in ten seconds. In less than a minute, Fatty is in full cardiac arrest. An unhealthy lifestyle kills.

I'm back to Ginger's feed. He's tentatively sniffing an open jar. Not good, it seems; someone's picky. There are more jars lined up in the cabinet—this should keep him occupied for at least a couple of minutes.

I run across the yard and jump over the kindergarten's fence. Using a shrubbery for cover, I reach the gazebo.

Top Dog is still clutching a small brown box in his left hand. It has two buttons—a standard-issue Chinese initiator.

Hand it over; it's mine now. I press the [Arm] button: a green LED lights up. Next to Top Dog's right hand rests a phone broadcasting Ginger's feed. No thanks—I'm already watching that movie.

Barehead carries an enormous open jar to the window, chomping on a pickle.

"Guys, I found some cucumbers. Fucking delicious!"

He sticks his find through the window, only to see Fatty sprawled on the ground below. Involuntarily, his hands let go of the jar. Bummer; what if they were actually good?

"Sorries, Ginger."

I press the button.

There was a good reason an RPG round was tucked in Ginger's pocket. It's a well-known live-bait tactic employed by gavriks: one unfortunate soul goes scouting the territory while his pals watch the feed on a phone screen. The chances of a lone blockhead surviving an encounter are abysmally low. The plan is that whoever makes the kill will also search the victim. At that point, they detonate the concealed grenade, potentially damaging the adversary. One final use of a dead friend's body. It sounds macabre, but the survival chances of a gavrik in the gray zone are pretty slim as it is.

The explosion is captured from different angles by both of my drones. The head, detached from the body, whirls out the window, its helmet camera still rolling. It draws a high arc in the air. At its peak, the centrifugal force separates the head from the helmet. Both objects hit the ground at roughly the same time. The helmet bounces a few times, rolls, and comes to rest at a perfect angle for the miraculously still-functioning camera to focus on the slightly dumbfounded face of ~~Ginger~~ Barehead.

And the Academy Award for Best Cinematography goes to… Barehead. *Post mortem.*

[End live]

[2]

On October 24th, 2024, russian fürer-wannabe-peter-the-great, issued the order to attack Ukraine. The early days of the war looked grim. It appeared like the nation might get crushed by the sheer force of the adversary. Against all odds and predictions of many, the valiant descendants of Cossacks mobilized, put up a fight, and drove the invaders out from large swathes of the occupied territory. The *second army in the world*[1] had to retreat embarrassingly, leaving behind both their personnel and equipment. At that moment, it seemed like the victory for Ukraine was within grasp.

Unfortunately, during the lull in fighting due to the harsh winter of 2023, the russians dug in, fitted themselves with dragon teeth[2], and amassed personnel and weapons. A Ukrainian counter-offensive launched in the spring of 2023 failed. The western military aid was too sluggish in arriving, meanwhile the russians learned their bitter lessons. Consequently, the Commander-in-Chief of the Armed Forces of Ukraine Valerii Zaluzhnyi had to acknowledge that the situation resulted in a deadlock.

Over time, the simmering conflict saw a diminishing role of traditional weaponry—artillery, tanks, and aviation. The distance between infantry front lines was growing, while the gray zone—a no-man's land nobody had a fair grip on—expanded to tens of kilometers. A new form of combat emerged—drone warfare. Ultimately, the units operating in the gray zone were primarily small teams of drone operators.

In 2024, the Western nations were still bickering over military aid, which was consistently being interrupted. The aggressor had their own problems, too—equipment stocks were dwindling, meanwhile the sanctions, albeit slow to being imposed, were just

1   A narrative from the russian propaganda of their armed forces being second only to the U.S. Since their shameful failures in Ukraine, the slogan became somewhat an object to mockery.

2   A fortification consisting of concrete cones, used to halt or slow down the advance of tanks and other heavy machinery.

starting to make a dent. At the end of the summer, ZSU[1] invaded russia and captured a significant portion of land in the Kursk region.

In 2025[2], a cease-fire negotiation led to a conditional truce: an immediate ban of medium and long-range rockets, as well as withdrawal of the heavy artillery. The ever-expanding gray zone continued to serve as the area of operations for drone teams from both sides.

Since the onset of the war, footage from surveillance drones, and later from the FPV[3] drones, gained massive popularity on social networks. The videos typically showed spectacular explosions caused by drone-released ordnance, destroying enemy soldiers or equipment worth millions. However, most social networks began clamping down on such content due to its extreme cruelty.

In 2025, a Warvid.Zone project was launched—a Youtube-TikTok clone, dedicated exclusively to visual material from the warzone. It came with all the essential attributes of a social network, including followers, likes, and comments, but none of the shackles on graphic content. Project owner—unknown. Its servers were scattered around the world's most obscure countries.

The first users to experience success on the platform were agents-editors. They would buy raw footage directly from soldiers, edit it, prop it up with music and commentary, then release it via their own channels. By the end of 2025, Warvid boasted a staggering five-million users. With all of them paying a monthly fee videos were effectively being converted into profits.

However, the biggest break for the new network came with the introduction of live streaming. Soldiers with popular channels were offered free equipment—a level IV ballistic helmet with an

1 Armed Forces of Ukraine.
2 This book was written at the end of 2024. Events described from this point on are the result of the author's imagination.
3 First Person View.

integrated communication system, two cameras (one regular and one night-vision), as well as a Starlink internet uplink, hooked up to both the helmet and drone cameras.

There was no shortage of those who wanted to sign up, and the army brass turned a blind eye to the activity—can't say no to a free helmet and a Starlink. Before long, live-streaming soldiers took over the agents in popularity. At the end of each broadcast, the editors, and in some cases even AI[1], would transform the raw footage into dazzling mini-movies that would continue to gather views and generate additional revenue for its creators.

When the project managers decided to make the income information public, all hell broke loose. Each streamer had a counter, indicating their proceeds, and the ones from the Top 10 were raking in as much as 200 thousand dollars a month.

Warvid was swamped with applications to join its streamer ranks.

There were only two main requirements:

- Actual combat experience or a completed military education.
- An applicant must travel to Ukraine on their own, as well as enlist in its foreign legion or another military unit.

Suddenly, ZSU experienced an influx of highly motivated recruits.

Eventually, russians came up with their own flawed but functioning Warvid clone. In the spring of 2026, something very significant happened that would later change the course of this war—the russian counterpart, along with all of its users, was incorporated into the original Warvid.Zone. The move stirred up a whole storm of outrage—*How is this possible? They're the aggressors after all*—but was outright ignored by the still *incognito* project managers.

Shortly after, a new set of rules was revealed:

20% of streamer's proceeds are to be collected and held in escrow by the network. Those funds are to be released only when a person decides to permanently leave Warvid.

....
1   Artificial Intelligence.

If a streamer was captured by someone from the opposing side—whether working alone or as part of a team—they would immediately forfeit their accumulated money in favor of their captor, provided they released the hostage and supplied video proof of the whole experience.

Upon their release, the captive's right to live-stream would be suspended for six months. While their previously created content could still generate revenue, all of it would go to the captor.

Besides this main rule, there were a few others:

- Teams could not exceed 4 persons.
- Hostages could not be tortured.
- Injured hostages must be provided with necessary medical assistance.
- Upon release, the captive must be allowed to reach a safe zone.
- Etc.

The rule changes transformed Warvid into a real-life *Battle Royale* or *Fortnite*.

By 2028, most of the soldiers operating in the gray zone were Warvid members. The rest were mockingly called gavriks.

[3]

My name is Martynas. I'm a 49 year old Lithuanian.

As a volunteer fighter, I've been involved in the war for Ukraine since 2014—mostly in reconnaissance and diversion units. During those years, I did what I had to do: I manufactured explosives, mined roads, installed traps, blew things up, fired Stingers and Javelins. However, my primary focus was on drones—scouting, dropping grenades, and flying suicide FPVs. Over time, I got very good at fixing and improving them. The modifications I came up with have been adopted in mass production of drones by Ukrainian and Lithuanian manufacturers.

Ukrainians gave me a new name—Master (Майстер)—not only in recognition of my technical expertise. With hundreds of fly hours under my belt—both in combat and in simulators—I was second to none in this particular art.

I'm a member of Ukraine's streamer legion. Commanders pass down assignments to me, and I see them through. I stream, but I'm not in it for the money—I got more than I need already. All my Warvid profits go towards Ukraine's restoration efforts.

On March 12, 2028, a russian explosive-carrying FPV drone crashed through the window of the cellar we were holed up in, killing two of my teammates. The section of my left arm was torn off below the elbow. I lost consciousness and would have surely bled to death if not for the automated experimental tourniquet that ultimately saved my life.

The war had ended for me—or so I thought.

X @eatontusk:
Hello, Master. I have a proposition.

"Your Margarita, Mr. Master."

A flight attendant, bearing a striking resemblance to Margot Robbie, offers me a tray with a meticulously prepared drink.

Besides the flight crew, I'm the only passenger on a Gulfstream G650ER Eaton sent to pick me up. The view outside gets a bit dull after crossing Scandinavia, and a few more margaritas later, I'm fast asleep. By the time I wake up, we're somewhere over Canada. For lunch, I order a burger and a cola, which feels fitting since I'm heading to America.

With an hour left to go, I hop into a luxurious shower, shave, and change into a fresh set of clothes. I'm ready to meet the world's richest person.

Brainlink corp., just one of Eaton's many endeavors, was working on something what futurologists were calling the next stage in the evolution—a human-computer hybrid. Its primary objective was quite noble: restoring mobility to disabled people by replacing signals of damaged nerves with digital ones. Nonetheless, there was little doubt that Tusk's long-term goal was far more ambitious—enabling interaction with computers, phones, and other devices directly from the human brain. After several years of testing the technology on animals, the company began implanting the first brainlinks in human volunteers in 2024.

The patients learned to control computer mice and keyboards using just their mind. Unfortunately, not everything was going smoothly. A few failures led Brainlink into a slew of lawsuits. Eaton announced a suspension of new implants while a much more advanced version was being developed. The company went quiet.

The meeting with the billionaire lasted just three minutes. He conveniently freed himself from useless small talk and other formalities by announcing that he had Asperger's syndrome. That suited me just fine—I feel like I might have a bit of that myself.

"You're getting a new arm—just like the Terminator. It's controlled via our next-generation brainlink. The best part, though, is that you won't need it to operate your drones or other devices. Frankly, arms won't be necessary for that anymore—you'll use your new brainlink to issue commands directly from your brain. Isn't it the most fucking awesome thing ever?"

After a bit more babbling about future potential, Eaton turned me over to his scientists:

"They'll explain everything. I have to take off. Bye!"

[7]

"Atari Hunter, CSO[1]."

The name, a slightly darker skin hue, and straight black hair alluded to some form of Japanese heritage. However, just like the iconic namesake computer brand, the scientist had no connections to the land of the sakura.

Her parents—both Americans and avid console computer fans—met in 1984 at a gamer event. They named their daughter Atari. The traces of Native American roots in her father's lineage may be reflected in her appearance. If I'm being totally honest, she looked just wow. Even a faint scar, partially concealed by an eyebrow, looked more like a curious tattoo or a quirky makeup style than a sign of an old injury.

Brainlink V2 fundamentally differed from its predecessor. The hole for the electrodes connecting to the brain was no longer being drilled in the vertex area. It was now discreetly located behind the ear. The number of electrodes increased from fifteen hundred to almost ten thousand. They were now connected to the auditory nerves as well, enabling two-way audio communication with a computer and eliminating the need for a screen. Almost all of the ear cartilage was replaced with an artificial one that housed a microcomputer and a battery. The two magnetic charging contacts were disguised as stud earrings.

The new hand had five fingers, which was about the extent of its similarities with the metal Terminator hand that Eaton had promised me. I guess the designers of this model were inspired by newer films.

Atari slipped a computer-connected glove onto her left hand. The artificial hand sprang to life, flawlessly mirroring her gestures without any noticeable delay. I would have loved to give it a try myself, but, coincidentally, I lacked that specific appendage.

----

1   Chief Scientific Officer.

"We'll print the artificial skin to match your skin tone—nobody will be able to tell the difference."

After the laboratory, I was kicked over directly to lawyers. The essence of the agreement was conveniently laid out in a TL;DR[1] section: they would install a brainlink and a hand, and I would agree with all the possible consequences, including death. By the time I reached page two, I realized I was already scanning for an **[Agree]** button.

"What are the odds of success?"

"We estimate those at 95%, but…"

The probability of everything working out well in a war is likely less than 5%.

"Acceptable."

Medical evaluation, surgery, and mastering the new devices—it took me a full two months.

Eaton himself arrived to see me off:

"Are you happy?"

"Yes, thank you."

"So, what's next?"

"I'll… BE BACK."

"I was expecting that answer."

He chuckled and left.

---

1   Too long; Didn't read.

I search the bodies and backpacks of the two dead gavriks. Several MREs[1] (no thanks, I don't eat that russian crap), and two power banks: one empty, the other almost full. I stash the latter into a pocket on my tactical belt.

Fully juiced batteries are likely the main prerequisite for surviving in the gray zone. Everything relies on a source of energy: transport, drones, cameras, Starlink, helmet visor, electronic jamming device, brainlink, and yes—my robot hand. Wall outlets don't work here, and the Ukraine-controlled territory is way too far.

The afternoon nap was not just for recuperation—the fold-out solar panel is set up on the roof, charging batteries. I take off running toward it. Warvid doesn't reveal coordinates of the unfolding action, but anyone can easily deduce the precise location using basic AI image analyzer. I'm sure that in an hour or two this place will be crawling with russian streamers and even more gavriks. It's time to put as much distance between myself and here as possible.

I quickly drop into the bedroom to grab my backpack before heading to the top floor, where the rooftop access ladder is located.

I'm gathering my things when Crow's video pops up: four quad bikes are approaching from the North.

Distance: 2.2 km

ETA[2]: 2:35

Shit, that was quicker than I expected. Those gavriks must have been used as bait.

I can manage four, but the rest who will surely follow shortly are bad news. This location is compromised, so fuck it:

[Start live]

---

1   MRE: Meal-ready-to-eat—military field rations.

2   Estimated time of arrival.

Taking several steps at a time, I reach the ground floor. Parked in the hallway of apartment No. 3 is a custom-made electric mountain bike—my sole means of transport and main battery guzzler. I slam the powerbank in: **battery level: 43%; approx. distance: 33 km**. One can live with that. I push the bike out into the stairway.

ETA: 00:23

There goes my chance to slip out undetected.

[9]

Normally, I would spend two to three weeks in the gray zone, then would return to civilization. An electric bike is the logical choice. A gas-powered motorcycle or a quad bike is suitable only for much shorter missions—there's no petrol here, whereas electricity can be generated. Worst case, I can pedal. A bike is silent, its acceleration is superb, and (presumably) it makes Greta Thunberg happy.

After I bounce down the final flight of stairs and burst outside, my new friends are right on top of me—less than a hundred meters away. I can hear the engines revving.

The street is riddled with potholes left by exploded mines, burnt-out vehicles, and other random debris. The only way my pursuers can move is in a single file, which means only their leader is currently taking potshots at me. Shooting from such a distance while using the other hand for steering is a waste of ammo—it would take Chuck to hit the target.

Warvid rules did not suddenly make everyone act civilized, cease using deadly weapons, or preserve life by, for example, aiming for the legs. They merely increased your chances of not being murdered in cold blood by a shot to the head—at least not before determining whether you might still prove useful.

Weaving between obstacles, at a narrow section of the road, I pull a custom lever on the handlebar. A grenade drops from a pipe attached to the rear wheel fork. A red dot lights up on Crow's video feed. Fifteen seconds later, its position is aligned with the first pursuer.

The grenade detonates directly underneath the quad bike, causing it to perform an impressive triple somersault, clipping a lamp post in the process. If this were a movie, the pole would have fallen directly onto the following vehicle. The driver slams onto the roof of a long-abandoned Zhiguli[1]. He'll likely live.

---

1   Zhiguli (Жигули)—an old russian car brand from the soviet era.

I always do my homework before settling into a place for an extended period. The most important task is to plan the escape routes ahead of time. A few hundred meters ahead the street crosses a creek that runs through a deep ravine. The bridge over it has long been blown up, but a single beam is still there. I spotted it yesterday while scouting the area. I slow down to cross to the other side. Crow's feed shows the three dickheads coming to a halt. Four wheels are no good for driving on narrow beams.

Waving my middle finger, I bid them farewell.

`[End live]`

They would likely be able to find a place to cross the creek if they cared to look, but I know they won't. They're going back to their friend, who is taking a nap on the roof of an old car. I make Crow glide down, snatch it mid-air and clip it to my backpack in a single motion. Then, I flick the anti-drone jammer on—just in case.

I'm a kid spending the summer in the countryside with my grand-parents. There, in the shade of a willow tree by the river, I sit with my feet submerged in a cool stream. Curious tiny stickleback fish tickle me, but I'm using my bamboo rod to catch something bigger. A grasshopper, which I caught in a nearby field, serves as bait. There are no weights or floats—an insect must kick at the surface to attract fish. I certainly would if someone tried to pierce me like that. I can see a group of dark shapes approaching the bait. The hook needs to be set at the precise moment the fish takes it. I'm hauling in fish one after another, stopping briefly to catch more grasshoppers. With fingers stained yellow from hopper juice, I unhook the fish and toss them into a water-filled aluminum barrel.

"Martynas, lunch!"

I hear my grandma calling out to me. No, not now! I'm reeling in the biggest fish.

"Martin!"

For some reason she's not pronouncing my name right. It doesn't sound Lithuanian at all.

I'm still trying to cling to the dream, but I'm not a kid anymore.

"Martin!"

It's not my grandma. It's Atari—Brainlink CSO.

"Buzz off—I'm busy."

A mumble escapes through my parched mouth and sticky lips. The dream is now completely gone. I peel my eyes open.

"You ruined it."

"I can imagine. Our anesthesiologist is very good."

She offers me an open water bottle.

"You must be thirsty."

I'm about to reach for it with my right hand when Atari stops me.

"Try using the other one."

She nods towards my left.

I'm now fully aware of the time and place. I take a peek at my left arm. It's there! I feel its weight when I try to lift it—a sensation I thought was lost. I want to touch it, but Atari is still holding my right hand. She draws the bottle closer to me. I extend my hand and observe my palm making contact with the plastic, but there's no sensation of a touch —just a slight impulse of impact. Instead, I can feel it in my body. I'm thirsty, and I desperately want to take that damn bottle. My artificial palm clasps and crushes it, causing the water to erupt from it like a fountain and splash onto Atari.

"That's for wrecking the dream."

"It appears your brain is still intact, though."

She laughs out loud.

On her way out, she leaves a present—a *C-3PO* robot set from the *LEGO Star Wars* collection. Very funny, ha ha.

"Try to complete it in five days. It's an exercise."

I'm done in two and ask for another set—*Millennium Falcon*, which consists of 7,541 pieces. I've always wanted it.

[II]

A robot hand fits on like a regular prosthetic. A small pump sucks out the remaining air, making the appendage attach to the rest of the arm so firmly that it's impossible to remove—I tried. The artificial skin is tattooed with some tribal Maori pattern. It's the real deal—they even brought in an artist to extend the artwork to my actual arm. The connection line is now effectively invisible. By the way, I didn't cry, I think.

The hand has an entire computer crammed into it, communicating with the brainlink module in my ear via Bluetooth. Mechanical joints in the wrist and the fingers are moved by tiny motors and hydraulic tendons, producing gestures that seem indistinguishably natural. The battery can be charged via two contacts—identical to the ones in my ear. USB type-H(uman)—I designate a name to a future standard.

I can move my left hand at will. I don't even have to think about it—everything happens naturally: I spot an object I want to touch or grab, I do it. Just like I would with my proper right hand.

I can literally hear the touch now. Sensors installed in the fingertips and palm transmit faint vibrations to my ear, each with a distinct rhythm. The human brain is incredible—eventually, the actual vibrations are tuned out, and I start to perceive them as touch.

I can feel heat and cold, too. At the point where the artificial hand connects to my remaining natural arm, there's a segmented conductor shaped like a scaled-down version of a palm. Each segment adjusts its temperature based on the object being touched. And yes—if I tried to shove it into lava, a safety regulator would kick in.

I'm officially a cyborg.

[12]

The luxury of being able to use all ten fingers again was making me happy, but the additional features simply blew my mind. I could say "expanded", but it wouldn't sound as cool.

The computer in my hand can connect to any device that supports Bluetooth, Wi-Fi, or other communication protocol. I fire up a PC or a Mac, grab the mouse, select **[Add New Bluetooth Device]**. The list of available devices pops up:

Master keyboard

Master mouse

Pair—Accept

The poor, gullible computer thinks it's paired with a mouse or keyboard. It doesn't realize it's been possessed by me. I look at the screen, see the mouse cursor, and think about where I want it to go or what buttons to press. I articulate words in my mind. The cursor moves, the buttons get pressed, the words appear. I articulate **format c:**[1] —be afraid!

It doesn't work on the first go—it takes a lot of training. The principle is simple: I start moving the mouse with my natural right hand (I'm right-handed). When a signal sounds, I stop the motion but continue it in my mind. The first efforts are chaotic, and progress is slow. Fortunately, I'm not the only one learning. An immensely powerful AI analyzes my brain signals, summarizes them, and feeds the data back to the hand's computer. I make exponential progress.

---

1   A command line command on DOS or Windows computers that would format (erase) their main disk.

The process is repeated for the keyboard, phone, and drone controller. With each new attempt, it takes progressively less time.

The hand's computer can also be connected to a screen, with the best option being glasses that project images directly onto their lenses. They are minimalistic, featuring a discreet projector in one temple and a camera in the other.

I can do a lot without a screen, too. For example, I can order Spotify to play *Moby* radio or ask ChatGPT, *Who the fuck is Alice?*[1] with the answer dictated directly into my ear, explaining something about wonderland (wrong answer). The list of commands isn't finite—I can create new ones at will to perform any task. I activate the **[Game Over]** command whenever I meet Atari—it plays Pac-Man's death sound on my phone.

Speaking of which, I no longer need a phone—there's an integrated GSM module. I carry it anyway, maybe out of habit, but more likely just to annoy Atari.

The possibilities are endless. I could effortlessly win *Jeopardy!*, *Who Wants to Be a Millionaire*, or any other show. I could count cards in Blackjack. Sadly, they said I'm not allowed to—it's all in the fine print.

....
1   A cover of the song *Living Next Door to Alice* by Smokie.

There's no mistake—the city I just escaped from shares a name with the world's most famous megapolis. Besides this curiosity, there were a few others: the street with the collapsed bridge was called *Freedom Lane (Волі провулок)*, and the bridge crossed a creek titled *Iron Ravine (Залізна балка)*, though a better translation for the word *балка* would be *beam*.

The names appear on the map projected onto my visor. I can't go deep south—the gray zone ends within a few kilometers, leading into the russian-controlled Donetsk region. To the east—Mordor is even closer. The logical choice would be to head west, toward Ukraine. However, the flaw in this plan is that it's too predictable. What's worse, I have the *Crooked End (Кривий торець)* river separating me from the West. The bridges are all destroyed, and the obvious crossing points are well known—the likelihood of finding my own crooked end there is strong.

After riding one and a half kilometers toward Donetsk, I turn east. A few crossroads later, I'm outside the city. There's a cemetery there; beyond it lie sprawling farmlands—no longer cultivated and heavily scarred with artillery craters. I pass by a long, narrow cluster of trees that Ukrainians call *posadka*, then turn left—back north.

I have a purpose for being here—at the edge of the gray zone. There are no Ukrainian streamers here, and not just because it's close to orc[1] territory. Several months ago, friendly streamers started disappearing in this area, leaving no trail or bounty requests. They'd just vanish.

If one streamer goes missing—OK, shit happens. Except there were three—all from Top-20. The Legion sent a four-man team composed of its most seasoned soldiers to investigate, only for them to vanish without trace, too. No more volunteers came forward.

....

1   Ukrainian people have a universally popular nickname for russian
    soldiers—orcs.

42

That's when I came back, complete with all my new toys. The commander asked me, almost jokingly: *Would you like to take this on?*

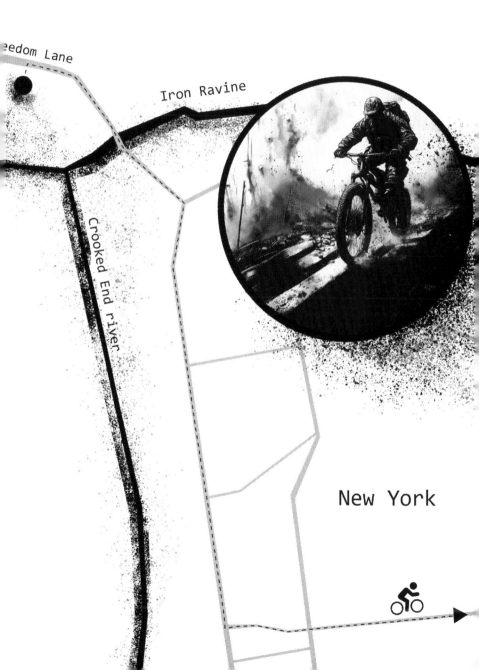

Freedom Lane

Iron Ravine

Crooked End river

New York

It takes me two hours to reach an abandoned coal processing plant in Pivden (Південне). The distance to it, as the crow flies, is eight kilometers. I covered nineteen. Getting around in the gray zone is painfully slow. Constantly scanning my surroundings with drones and my own eyes, I work to evade minefields and potential ambushes, as well as to find suitable crossing points on rivers and creeks. I avoid people, too.

I scrutinize the area where I'm about to hole up. I examine the buildings using drones—not just from the outside, but also by flying inside them whenever possible. Did I miss anything? It's time to go in and check for myself.

The plant was abandoned back in 2014, but since there has been no active fighting here, the whole complex is in reasonably good condition. Nature has started to reclaim the area, though—concrete is covered with moss, small trees sprout on roofs and from every crack where they can find a grain of soil. Vines envelop buildings, pipes, and other structures. It would make a perfect setting for an episode of *The Last of Us*.

It's already dusk when I ride into the territory. It's quiet, but I can hear leaves rustling and roofing materials clattering in the wind. I can almost feel the fungi-controlled zombies watching me from every nook and cranny.

Yuck! I don't need this right now.

I take up residence on the first floor of the administrative building. I'm the manager of this plant now, or so claims a dangling plaque that says *Director*. A long hallway links twelve rooms—six on each side. At the southern end, there's an entrance to a skybridge that connects to the production facility.

I use a cabinet to barricade the window, leaving a small gap for observation, which I cover with a piece of glass. This setup should obscure my heat signature from thermal cameras and provide extra warmth.

I install transparent tripwires across the doorways of all entrances. Tripping one would trigger a directional anti-personnel mine. Then, I head up to the roof to set up the Starlink—it's useless indoors—as well as the water collector.

I'm back in the manager's office. A couch would be nice, but there isn't one—it must've been part of my predecessor's severance package. I pull out my inflatable mat. It comes with a special pouch for inflating: trap air inside, seal the open end, and push the air in. Instead, I use my mouth—it leaves me feeling a little buzzy. Just a small bit of fun to brighten the day.

During the day, it warms up to +10°C[1], but by dawn, temperatures will drop close to freezing. I'm dressed lightly—a single thermal base layer, along with Gore-Tex pants and a jacket. If the advertising is to be believed, I could soak in the shower for three days straight and stay perfectly dry, though I haven't tested that claim. Over my jacket, I wear a bulletproof vest and nothing else—it would make me heat up, sweat, and dehydrate faster during physical activity.

Still, when it's freezing outside and there's nothing to do, the thought of an extra sweater creeps in. To be fair, I have my own heating system—a warm-up mesh sewn into my base layers. But guess what it runs on? Yes, charged batteries, which makes it a no-go. Instead, I take out a sleeping bag and roll it out on the mat.

It's too early for sleep—anxiety won't let me. No, it's not because of the zombies. It's more like the feeling a nicotine addict experiences when they know there are only two cigarettes left and no store around. The total remaining charge across all my batteries is a mere 12.3%. The forecasts predict crappy weather—three days of heavy rain. I won't be able to squeeze anything out of the solar collector, even if I try.

I'll need to find a creative workaround. After all, I'm the manager of this establishment.

Solar energy is the most accessible way to obtain power in the gray zone—when it's available. In the fall, as the days get shorter,

1   10C = 50F.

the number of active fighters here dwindles dramatically. During winter, only the absolute psychos remain—there's less sun, and batteries drain much faster in cold. Not to mention, you also need to keep yourself warm.

In perfect conditions, the solar panel can charge all the power banks in four hours. Add another four for the bike. However, since ideal conditions are seldom available, fully charged batteries are a rare luxury.

The only alternative that is always readily available is pedals. I can turn on the charging while riding (though with all the weight I carry, it wouldn't feel like a leisurely weekend outing), or I can do so while at a standstill. I just have to suspend the rear wheel, switch on the transformer, and charge away. Well, not exactly away—I'm staying put.

It takes eighteen hours of feet wiggling to fully juice up all the batteries. I can only manage about four hours of that per day—I'm not Lance Armstrong, after all. As a side effect, this particular form of entertainment requires another source of energy: nutrition. Newton's law of energy transformation in effect.

Just over 10% of the remaining capacity is bad news. It's draining even when I'm at rest. Both Magpie and Crow are perched on the windowsills (one in the window I barricaded, the other in the room across), constantly filming and analyzing the surroundings. A frequency spectrometer is searching for hostile drones and other sources of radio signals. Even devices on standby are slowly sipping energy.

I eat an MRE, then hop on the bike and start pedaling.

I log into Warvid.Zone. The video of my escape is ranked first. In third place is my run-in with the gavriks. As for the second—let's just say I'm the lead star in it.

[15]

You're probably familiar with at least one movie where lovers are so inseparable they can communicate telepathically, even over long distances. That's level 9000 romance right there.

In short, Atari and I have something similar.

The Robotaxi is taking me to the airport. Driverless rides have the added convenience of not having to make small talk. I'm free to think whatever I want. I think about Atari.

"I'm going to miss you."

Did I actually hear that, or was it just my imagination? The voice feels distant, coming from deep inside my head.

What was that?

Is the farewell champagne finally kicking in?

Or maybe it's a side effect of the surgery?

Somewhere over the Atlantic, I give up, and message Atari:

"You did that, didn't you?"

I see her typing a reply. It takes way longer than it would for a simple *What?*. Nevertheless, the answer is short:

"Yes."

"How?"

It turns out I allowed Brainlink scientists to keep a backdoor to my hand's computer when I signed the agreement. Officially, it's for bug fixing, deploying version updates, as well as monitoring the hand's data and my vitals.

Apparently, Atari received a signal about a small anomaly when I left.

"Your pulse was above the regular range. It would be quite normal for anyone else, but your heart is steady, even in stressful situations. I downloaded and analyzed the logs. If you want to write something out, you need to clearly form the words and articulate them—you know the drill. I can see those words in the log… Whoa, your pulse is shooting up again."

No shit.

"Ummmm…."

"No worries. The only recognizable word was my name. You were repeating it pretty persistently."

"It's a fragment from a Lithuanian folk song. I always get agitated when I'm singing—it reminds me of my grandma."

In short, I'm an idiot for not bothering to read the full agreement. It states that Brainlink is monitoring me 24/7. Fortunately, I do have the option to turn on privacy mode.

Atari claims the feeling is mutual, it's just that I, being a complete dumbass, did not realize it. She didn't make the moves either, as it would have been a violation of company policies. Even that small message directly to my head was grossly illegal.

From then on, we talk constantly. Not just talk—we watch movies, play chess, and engage in brain games like *Alias* and others. Before long, this evolves into a surreal new kind of shared life. Atari is the number one recipient of Brainlink V2—she just couldn't ask others to commit to something she hasn't tried herself.

The **[Hello, Atari]** command launches a dedicated app. The notes that Atari sends me (that she forms in her mind, just like I do) are read out by artificial intelligence directly into my ear, in her voice and intonation. My messages reach her in exactly the same way.

Atari avoids watching my broadcasts from Ukraine. By mutual agreement, I don't share much about what's happening here—she prefers it that way.

[Privacy mode: ON]

For the past year, Davai Lama[1] has been the most popular russian streamer. Bulky and ugly, he bore a striking resemblance to ex-boxer and State Duma member Valuev—not just in his hideous face but also in his physique. He did a lot of sports, consumed even more alcohol, and could eat anything. Considered himself immortal. After downing a bottle of vodka, he would simply burp and shout: *I'm a bear!!!*

One day, pancreatitis almost got him. A month spent in a hospital marked the first time he was sober since early teens. There, in the patient room someone lent him a book—*Practical buddhism and meditation*. The latter came naturally—he did not have a lot of stray thoughts to get in the way.

"I'll be Buddha."

He decided.

After recovering, he rounded up his old pals, banned alcohol, and returned to the gray zone. He changed his Warvid username to Davai Lama. Before his ordeal, he had barely ranked within the top two hundred. Now that he was sober, he could take on more challenging tasks. More importantly, he started streaming regularly. The ranks of his followers grew, propelling him all the way to first place.

The video currently sitting in second place is his.

I watch the video filmed from another perspective. As Lama lands on the roof of a car, the view switches to the camera of the colleague who was following him. Just as I assumed, after my escape via the collapsed bridge, they returned to their boss. Davai Lama comes into view, sitting on the roof of that same car, smoking.

"You OK?"

"Yes. I'm gonna kill that cunt."

---

1 Davai Lama—sarcastic transliteration of the title of Tibethan spiritual leader—Dalai Lama. "Davai" translates to "C'mon" from Russian.

I guess he wasn't paying full attention to the writings in his book on Buddhism after all.

I watch the video again, noting what weapons and equipment my pursuers are using.

After two hours of pedaling, my energy storage is at 22%.

Bedtime. I'll use my sleeping bag as a blanket—it would take too long to get out of it in case of an emergency.

[18]

I wake up fifteen seconds before the alarm sounds, as always. It's still dark outside, drizzling. A sixth, or maybe even seventh sense tells me I'm not alone in the room. I flip on the night vision and look around: two rats are sniffing for leftovers. I prop myself up, which makes Chip and Dale scuttle away.

In the heat of the war, all possible areas were completely crapped over with landmines. Now that the fighting has scaled down, no new ones are being laid—there's no way for streamers to bring them in. When navigating around the gray zone, we have the option to report spotted mines in, just like mobile map app users report police patrols or road accidents. All movements are tracked, too. The data—delayed by a few days—is used to generate a map of places that can be considered somewhat safe.

Here's how it works: a streamer, traversing through the gray zone, paints a virtual thin semi-transparent line. If someone walks the same route, their line is overlaid on the previous one. The more people successfully walk there, the more prominent the specific track gets.

Besides marking safe routes, the lines also indicate their popularity. By comparing the most recent version of the map with older ones, I can deduce when the zone of interest had visitors (excluding the last few days).

I chose this plant for a reason—hardly anyone ever visited it. The last new lines were dated two weeks ago. Interestingly, one of the missing Ukrainian streamers passed through here about a month ago. With luck, I might pick up some clues. It's a bit naive of me to think that way—at this moment, I'm a small fish being hunted by a pike. I just hope I'm big enough to get choked on.

I slowly and thoroughly survey the territory, noting every detail and trying to imagine how the enemy would act. I designate the places to mine. All the pieces of junk lying around get inspected and assessed for possible uses. I keep coming up with possible scenarios—often fatal for me. Everything I see goes on camera, too—I'll review it again while resting.

I position cameras at strategically important spots. They take a snapshot every few seconds and compare it with the previous one. If any significant change is detected, they switch to live mode and notify me of a potential threat. The hardware itself is similar to that of a drone: a directional camera, a video transmitter, and a receiver for control signals. Everything is disguised as construction debris—stuffed into scraps of sealant or latex foam.

Now that the reconnaissance is done, I head northeast—the road between the workers' quarters and another nondescript building is marked as mined. Approaching it, I see two craters left by explosions. I get Crow airborne to take thermal snapshots of the surface.

Shallowly buried mines retain heat longer in the evening and cold in the morning, which makes them somewhat discernible. It's not the most reliable method, especially when it's raining or there's no sun out, but it'll have to do.

I scrutinize the surface for signs that might reveal the locations of the explosives, comparing them with thermal shots. Ten meters ahead, I notice a small depression. Before taking each step, I probe the ground for mines with a long knife specifically designed for the task. I do it again when I reach the designated spot—gotcha. I repeat the motion a few more times, feeling out its edges.

There's a saying among professional deminers: Know how to spot the mines, but don't touch them. I'm going to ignore it this time.

Kneeling, I use a small shovel to slowly dig a ditch around the mine. Cautiously, I brush it clean: a russian anti-tank TM-62 explosive device, encased in metal and weighing around 9 kilos.

On my side, I form a sloping ramp in the dirt. I take out a hooked carbon rope, loop it around the mine, and secure it back to itself. After retracing my steps to a safe zone, I take cover behind a concrete block and start to pull slowly on the rope. Roughly one in fifty mines has a present hidden underneath it—another explosive. Just grabbing it would be foolish.

I mine potential routes of the enemy, convenient cover spots, and entrances to buildings. Some explosives are buried, while others are set up to be detonated remotely. I mark them on the map—I'll upload that data when (or if) I bug out of this place. I don't need the emotional burden of accidental deaths.

I repeat this procedure eight times, spending almost an hour each time. Time for rest.

On the way to my temporary residence, in a copse of birch trees, I stock up on wild boletuses and orange-caps, leaving the russulas for the worms. Calories are my favorite dish.

Mushrooms are not the only things I find under the trees—rabbit droppings are there as well. I set some snares.

I climb up onto the roof to replace the full rainwater container with an empty one.

Dinner menu: chicken cutlet from an MRE and mushroom soup made with a bouillon cube. I finish it off with a chocolate chip cookie for dessert.

I'm back in the saddle, pedaling.

[19]

"Tell me the story behind the eyebrow scar."

"You noticed, huh? Believe it or not but your fellow countryman is to blame."

"Who? I need to have a talk with him."

"Ha ha. My father grew up in Santa Monica. He was buddies with Natas Kaupas…"

"OMG. The skater?"

"You know him? Is he famous down there?"

"Nah, I think he's known to very few. When I was a child, there were about twenty decent skaters in Vilnius. Good boards were hard to come by—we had to assemble our own from spare parts. The parents of my schoolmate were kind of well-off during *Perestroika*[1]; they could go abroad. One day, they brought me Natas Kaupas' board and a videotape of his film."

"*Streets of Fire*?"

"Yes. We watched it hundreds of times over, trying to replicate the tricks."

"Well, he taught me those himself."

"Amazing… We used to copy Natas' logo on our boards. We were so proud that one of America's most famous skaters was Lithuanian. It's the mentality of a small nation—even now, everyone is overjoyed when some celebrity is revealed to have a speck of Lithuanian heritage. So, you got the scar from skating?"

"Yes. I attempted his famous fire hydrant spin. Did you know how to do it?"

....

1   Perestroika—political and economic reforms initiated in the
     Soviet Union during the 1980s under Mikhail Gorbachev, aimed
     at restructuring the economy and encouraging more openness and
     transparency in governance.

"Nope. We didn't have hydrants back then."

"Natas would not let me do it—he said I wasn't ready. But one day, I saw one—bright yellow—on my way to school. I just couldn't resist the invitation to jump and spin on it. I managed the ollie, but the board slipped away, and I banged my head on the hydrant. I woke up in a hospital with a concussion and stitches above my eye. Doctors wanted to make sure I didn't have internal bleeding, so they kept me there while awaiting the results of my head MRI. I was lying in bed, watching countless section views of the brain in my test report, thinking about how all the knowledge and thoughts can fit in there."

"Then Natas is responsible not just for the scar but for your career as well?"

"Seems that way."

"You didn't give up skating, did you?"

"I didn't. My parents made me wear a helmet, though."

We watch *Streets of Fire*, constantly pausing to reflect on the past. Atari tells stories about Natas. I'll ask for an introduction the next time I'm in California.

[20]

My second day at the plant. The downpour is keeping Magpie and Crow grounded. I check the rabbit snare—empty. It's probably better this way; I always feel sorry for the poor trapped fella. I dismantle the trap and forage for some orange-caps instead—I can go vegetarian for a while (MRE chicken doesn't count).

With breakfast done, I venture out for an extensive inspection of the building. The cellar is flooded knee-deep. I thoroughly check all five floors, then make my way up to the roof. It's overflowing with water, too—all the drain pipes are clogged. I pedal, eat, and sleep for the rest of the day.

[21]

[Hello, Atari]

"Were you into video games as a child?"

"Sure. Go ahead, guess what the first computer I touched was."

"Ummm... Atari?"

"Right on. I knew then and there that my life had changed—I wouldn't be able to live without one. I was twelve. My older sister was taking art classes, and once she told me that the youth center where her art workshop was held had set up a few Ataris. I told my parents I wanted to enroll too. I arrived early, before the class started. They were all running the same game—*Montezuma's Revenge*."

"My fave!"

"Ten minutes would cost a ruble[1]—a week's worth of allowance! Two visits wiped out my savings—I had to lie that someone took the money from me. A new goal was born: earn enough money for my own comp. I bred parrots and goldfish and sold them at a local marketplace. I took pictures of Rambo and Terminator posters, made small black-and-white copies, then peddled them at school."

"So, breaking copyright laws."

"Those didn't exist in the Soviet Union. Once, our physics teacher demonstrated how a person's electrical current could be measured by attaching zinc and copper plates. We placed an ammeter inside a fancy box, decorated it with stickers, and gauged people's biofields at a local fair."

"Scammers! What did you tell them?"

"We measured ourselves plus a friend's mother, discussed how we felt, and approximated the conclusions."

....

1 Ruble—currency used in Russia and the Soviet Union. At the time Lithuania was occupied, hence the use of the currency.

"A rather small reference group. How did it go?"

"Not good. Fortunately, my father came up with a business idea that ultimately paid for my first computer. We used lamps to grow a thousand tulips in our small apartment, aiming for them to bloom on March 8th—the International Women's Day. In the Soviet Union, a man who didn't bring home flowers on that day risked forfeiting his dinner or a head injury by a dough roller. We left for Minsk the day before, and by morning, we were sold out."

"Why Minsk?"

"Because it was close, and tulips were selling for twice as much there."

"So, you bought an Atari then?"

"No, they didn't take root here. I bought a clone of the Sinclair ZX Spectrum, in parts: a plain board, microchips, etc. Collecting all the components alone took half a year. I carried a list of missing parts to an electronics market every Saturday. The console was buggy but functioned, and I was happy."

"How old were you, again?"

"Thirteen. I then moved on to other ventures: copying games onto cassettes, designing game levels, and connecting computers to television sets for friends. The latter wasn't as easy as it sounds—I had to open up the TV and solder in a few extra components. The work had to be done when parents were not at home—who'd in their right mind let a teenager gut their equipment?!?"

"Master: The Beginning."

We play *Montezuma's Revenge*. Atari claims the first win, while I get stuck on the same levels I struggled with nearly four decades ago.

A warning wakes me: the spectrometer has detected a rogue frequency, most likely from a recon drone—a DJI or something similar. It's 4 a.m. and still dark—someone must have decided to take advantage of the lull in the rain to scout with a thermal camera.

I remain still, listening. In a matter of minutes, the hum of propellers reaches me. The drone's pilot is canvassing the territory, searching for heat signatures. Fortunately, the heating was shut off back in 2014. I didn't build a fireplace, and my body heat won't register from the outside since the window is barricaded. It's unlikely they'll risk losing the drone by flying into the building while it's still dark.

I take a stab at decoding the video signal. No such luck—the Chinese know their craft. After snooping for about half an hour, the drone takes off east. The signal vanishes—they must've turned it off or are changing the batteries. I tag the pilot's approximate position. Distance—300-400 meters. There's no second flyby, but presumably, it will continue in the morning.

I wish they'd just give up and fuck off. The batteries are empty, and escaping on a bike is a mission (almost) impossible. If I get involved in a conflict, everyone will know. I always activate silent mode before going to sleep—none of my devices emit any signals, making me effectively invisible on the frequency spectrum. I'm counting on getting through this without a drama.

Most likely, at dawn, they'll be back with one or more drones to check the building's interior. It will look suspicious if they can't access my room through both the window and the door.

I relocate to a nearby storage room, demoting myself from a manager to a janitor. The new real estate fits well with my updated status—a cramped space and no windows. I hang a detached door back on its hinges and eat an early breakfast—no telling when there will be another opportunity. Just before dawn, I visit the bathroom at the end of the hall. I stay below the windowsills by stooping when passing the office doors.

I have a problem.

A very shitty problem.

They sniffed me out. Quite literally.

Two drones showed up at first light. One began scanning from the ground floor up, while the other started from the top.

I pushed the door fully ajar for a few moments to equalize the temperature, threw on a thermo-reflective cloak, then closed the door again, leaving a gap too small for a drone to squeeze through. The hum from the one coming up from below grew louder. It lingered next to my slightly opened door before moving on to the manager's office. Systematically, it checked all the rooms one by one, popping into the bathroom at the end.

At that moment, I knew I had made a mistake.

In the dim light of the loo, they would most certainly turn on the thermal camera.

Did I take a dump there after breakfast? Yes.

Did I flush? No, because there's no water.

How long has it been? Half an hour.

Is the shit still warm? Yes, a bit.

Did I crap up my chances? Almost certainly, yes.

[24]

The drone darted out of the window and whirred toward the base, followed by the one from the upper levels. A slim chance remained that they had both run out of juice. If they returned to check the remaining floors, there would still be hope they missed my stinky clue.

Half an hour went by. The frequency spectrometer was still flat-lining; there was no hum from the propellers.

Fuck.

No point in hiding the radio signals anymore. I let Crow fly out the window, climbing high above the building—to about two hundred meters. The zoom on her camera is good enough that I don't need to fly directly towards the enemy. I aim in the general direction of where I think my visitors are holed up. A gap between two buildings, overgrown with trees, shows fresh sets of quad-bike tire tracks leading into it.

That you, Davai Lama?

I fly a few hundred meters east-west over the forest, then lower the drone to just above the treetops. I direct its camera towards the target building and zoom in. Two shapes can be seen behind the ground floor window—how do you do, comrades?

This exceptional courage needs to be exploited. I quickly whip up a plan: swoop in, fire a dart, and bug out.

There are a couple of tall trees in front of the window. Idiots—the foliage would provide perfect cover if they'd bother to get just one floor up. On the other hand, I won't be able to just lurch up after taking a shot—the branches are in the way— and it's too risky to go inside. I'll need to make a sharp turn to the right, between the trunks and the wall.

As I launch toward the targets, I see the third, much larger figure glimmer into view deeper in the room. Davai Lama it is.

Fuuuuuuuuuuuuuuuck! With only a few meters to go, I lose control of the drone. The spectrometer lights up with a slew of random signals. They've fired up the jammer.

Crow is returning—it's programmed to backtrack home after losing the signal. It must be a powerful jammer—I regain control only near my building. I guide the drone into the window, then ground it.

[25]

"Well, well, Master, you really made a shitshow, didn't you?"

A muted voice crackles over the common Warvid radio band.

I don't reply—there's no way to win this with words, and silence drives such numbskulls mad.

"Why don't you outright give yourself up? It'd save us time."

Right. Just a moment.

Two hours pass, and nothing happens. I'm back on my bike to resume the Tour de ~~France~~ Donbas.

A message from Z3N3K pops up:

"Hey. Got info for you: Davai Lama has assembled three groups and is offering a big bonus for your head. If they manage to capture you alive, the reward doubles. They're on their way. Counting his own boneheads, sixteen *pidars*[1] in total."

The reason behind the hold-up is now clear: they're waiting for backup to arrive. It's a bit scary to go in alone.

Z3N3K—a Ukrainian hacker who is constantly monitoring

----

1   The most common moniker for occupying russian soldiers, used in a super derogatory sense roughly translating as "fag", but without any homosexual undertone.

hundreds of open and private chat channels—notifies me the minute something important catches his attention. We're both members of the same unit—Ukraine's streamer legion.

"What's their take on the max four attackers rule?"

"They're supposedly attacking in fours. The rest are just lookouts in case you decide to bail out. But in reality, fuck knows? You know how rules are treated."

"Gotcha. Thanks."

"You owe me a beer when you get back."

[26]

Not good.

Pidars have had their jammer off for a while now (it gobbles up energy, so it would be foolish to have it on all the time). I get Crow flying over my building. An AI algorithm detects the motion before me—a group of quad-bikes is slowly advancing down the road to the west.

I compare the current view to the one from this morning. There are two new sets of tracks: one leads to a small house to the north, located at the base of a huge heap of coal refuse (distance—180 meters), and the other toward a group of structures to the south (240 meters) . Neither of those locations is directly visible from mine, which explains why the cameras did not register the new arrivals.

All that's left is to wait for the western group to settle in before the encirclement is complete.

[27]

Not good #2.

Suddenly Crow's video jolts to the side. A split second later I hear a bang of a shot (a bullet travels twice as fast as the sound). They shot my little birdie. Fucking assholes.

Crow is tumbling down—its video feed a blur of sky and ground—about to slam into the roof. A mere few meters away, I regain control and manage to land it.

The diagnostics show a damaged propeller. Trying to fly it through a window is too risky—wonky controls could make it hit something and cause even more damage. I'll have to go up there myself.

I rewind the recording. The impact kicked the drone south—the shot came from the north. The vantage point is obvious: one of the two heaps of coal waste, each towering up to forty meters. I'd go with the one on the right.

I task the AI with finding the shooter's location—maybe the recording caught a muzzle flash. No luck—the resolution is too low. I know I can't just stroll across the roof; the sniper is likely perched at forty meters, while the roof is only at fifteen. I'd be a sitting duck.

[28]

Not good #3.

I climb to the top floor. The narrow windows in the stairwell are made of thick glass blocks. Dirty and aged, they barely let any light through, allowing me to move without worrying about staying hidden. I step up onto the ladder but stop just short of peeking outside. Cautiously, I lift Crow off the ground and fly it toward the roof hatch—I need it close enough to snatch quickly.

The drone wobbles, moving like a drunk, forcing me to compensate for the damaged propeller. It turns out to be a blessing in disguise—two more sniper shots ring out as I try to cover the short distance. Good luck hitting a drunken Crow. They expected me to climb onto the roof myself, which explains why it hasn't been finished off while it was stationary.

I grab the wounded bird. A shattered propeller is a minor problem—I have plenty of replacements. Unfortunately, there's a much more serious issue: the dart gun is irreparably damaged.

[29]

Next to the three not-goods, there's a single good-good: before going up, I pointed Crow's north-facing camera at the peaks of the coal waste hills. Reviewing the footage revealed the shooter's precise location—Crow's abuser lurks atop the overgrown heap on the right—under a birch tree on its left slope.

Sniper is probably the most romanticized profession among warriors—a true introvert's dream. You skulk in relative safety, waiting. And waiting some more. You can wait for an eternity without eating, shitting, or pissing—you're that hardcore. With your target in the crosshairs, you factor in wind velocity and distance. You exhale half a lung of air, then steadily pull the trigger in a slow, controlled motion. You kill the enemy. You kill a lot of enemies, just like Simo Häyhä[1] during the Winter War. You vanish without trace. They spin legends about you and bestow a battle alias—White Death—because nobody actually knows your real name or has ever seen your face. What's not to like?

Yet, the reality of a war in Ukraine has diminished the significance of snipers—the front lines have moved too far apart for a bullet. The enthusiasts venturing out to hunt close to enemy lines wouldn't last long—the very first shot would be instantly followed by a greeting from artillery or suicide drone pilots.

1   A legendary Finnish sniper who singlehandedly shot over 500 russian soldiers during the Winter War (1939–1940).

Streamer skirmishes have made snipers relevant again. I now have to dispose of at least one of these romantics. Not just for revenge for Crow—as long as he's out there, I can't even poke my nose outside.

A sniper always tries to spot motion. If they have a thermal camera (who doesn't?), they also watch for thermal signatures. Knowing their position offers me no advantage—I can't just pop out to shoot—they're ready, and they'll fire first. I can watch the video feed, wait for them to answer nature's call, take aim, and stay put until they return. But what if the area is covered by another sniper? That's exactly how I would do it. Besides, ain't nobody got time for that.

[30]

Shooter's dispatch to the happy hunting grounds will have to wait. After all, they don't deserve that place.

I make my way down to collect the equipment. While rummaging in bike panniers, I receive a warning from the spectrum analyzer about a surge in signal activity. The cameras are getting agitated as well: drones are closing in from all four directions.

Streamers would often use recon drones to smoke out targets. A suicide FPV drone would be too difficult to control in a confined space. In contrast, a recon drone is equipped with sensors and stabilizers, allowing it to hover in place and navigate obstacles. It can also deploy mines fitted with wide-angle cameras. This restricts the target's movement inside the building—the explosion can be triggered by motion or remotely by an operator.

Thanks, but I'll pass—I switch the jammer on. The drones freeze, then turn and back off retracing their route. Two of them head straight back to their owners. The ones remaining put in some distance then begin to flail about unpredictably, clearly trying to avoid Crow's fate. Regardless, I'm not planning on shooting while at least one sniper is watching the building.

In half an hour, the drones scurry away to get their batteries changed. They are replaced by fresh ones that resume their mosquito jive.

This scenario keeps repeating. The jammer is constantly active, munching through my watt supply. I suspect that depriving me of power is part of their strategy.

The forecast keeps predicting shit weather: rain or overcast. I plop onto the bike—time to make some ampere-hours.

I task all cameras with locating the snipers. The raw footage is uploaded to a server where an AI takes over—my computer is not powerful enough for running such analysis.

[31]

[Hello, Atari]

I complain about the batteries.

"We'll install a mini atomic reactor into your hand. As soon as such a thing gets invented. You'll be able to power a small town with the leftover energy."

"Deal. Settlements here don't have any power. Wanna watch a movie?"

"What happened to conserving energy?"

"I'd rather be with you. Choose one?"

"How about… *And now ladies and gentlemen*? Starring…"

"Irons and Kaas. I'd love it."

I'm completely drained after three hours of continuous pedaling, with little to show for it. Damn jammer is always hungry. Oddly enough, I'm feeling quite cheerful.

As the downpour returns, the drones hastily flee. It's time to hunt the hunter.

[32]

I climb up to the top floor. The sniper sitting on the coal waste hill is visible only from two north-facing offices. I choose the left one, then sit on the floor next to the doorway, propped up against the wall of the hallway.

Shooting around corners is nothing new. There have been many attempts: elongated grips, mirrored contraptions, even curved barrels, no matter how idiotic it may sound.

My setup is different: a camera is attached to the rifle, along with a pull mechanism connected to its trigger. The camera transmits the view directly to my visor. The weapon itself is mounted on a tripod, which is equipped with small motors that allow me to raise, lower, and turn it. How? With my mind, of course.

I grab a discarded slab of wood and use it to slowly push the rifle stand toward the doorway—remember, the sniper is watching for motion. For once, the raging rain is on my side, creating a lot of visual noise. I take aim. Both the camera left on the windowsill and the one mounted on the rifle show the same view: a lonely birch tree sheltering a sniper covered in a masking net. Distance: 245 meters. The view is magnified 56 times. If it weren't for the rain and the net, I could describe the face in great detail.

The stand is not heavy—the recoil kicks the rifle back, causing the camera to lose sight of the target. I pull the whole contraption closer.

A slow-motion playback from the window camera reminds me of the *Sniper Elite* video games. They depict how the bullet slices through the enemy's internal organs, shatters bones, and causes blood to explode in spectacular spurts. The recording doesn't show all those details, but the rest is filled in by my vivid imagination.

One down (200[1]).

....

1   Package 200—an official designation of a KIA (killed in action) soldier in Russian millitary nomenclature.

[33]

While harvesting honey, Winnie-the-Pooh had a choice between a green and a blue balloon. The green one was supposed to help him blend in with the tree, while the blue one would resemble a patch of sky. He went with the latter.

Mine is green. Unlike *Bear of Very Little Brain*[1], I want my balloon to be noticeable.

I inflate it and stick it out through the doorway.

Nothing.

Stooping, I dart to the office window and offer the balloon up again.

Nothing.

I repeat the routine in the room facing west.

Nothing.

I empty the balloon and fill it up again, repeating the procedure on the southern side.

Nothing.

Eastern side.

A bullet lodges itself in the wall across from the window. The sound of the shot reaches my ears moments later. Minus one balloon.

The air in a balloon retains heat, making it stand out in a thermal camera, while its round shape might be mistaken for a helmet. No sniper would be able to resist the temptation.

I now know the location of the second shooter's hideout—the workers' living quarters to the east.

I set up the rifle next to another, farthest office. It takes a moment to locate the sniper's position. He's still looking through the scope

....

1   A. A. Milne's character Winnie-the-Pooh in the namesake childrens' book referred to himself as "Bear of Very Little Brain".

while speaking on the radio.

Bragging about the kill, huh?

Minus two, I think to myself, but stop short of pulling the trigger.

They're convinced they got me. It's raining—no way to use a drone. My bet is on someone coming to confirm the kill in person. I'll wait.

I leave the rifle trained on the sniper, biding my time.

In fifteen minutes, three figures emerge from behind the living quarters building. They slink, avoiding direct visibility by seeking cover behind bushes and structures. Their route follows the one I envisioned when I was laying the mines.

Only ten meters to go.

At the sound of the explosion, I activate the trigger mechanism. The shot is drowned out by the echo of the blast. I'm pretty confident it went undetected. The window camera is busy filming the action below, which means I have to reaim the rifle at the sniper's position to verify the result.

Minus two (200). For real this time.

In the video feed, I see two of the invaders knocked down by the explosion heaving themselves up. The third one remains on the ground—a missing leg makes getting up a bit complicated.

One would expect the two healthy chums to help their companion. To survive a severed leg injury, you need not only to be extracted to a safe zone and have a tourniquet applied, but also to be delivered to a hospital within hours. Nobody cares to do that in the gray zone. Your survival is your own business.

"We walked into a mine. Fuck."

Their cussing reaches me through the window. The leader is on the radio, communicating with the other groups. I can't hear what they're being asked, though—they're wearing headsets.

"Vovka and I are fine. Dumdum… Dumdum is toast."

"……..."

"Yes, dead."

He kneels next to the wailing Dumdum and wraps both hands around his neck. Minus three (200).

I aim my rifle at the Good Samaritan helping Dumdum ease his pain. I wait until he's finished. Minus four (200).

The remaining russian lurches toward the nearest corner. Even if I manage to hit him, it's probably not fatal (300[1]?).

The reports of my death are greatly exaggerated[2].

Half an hour goes by.

"Master, I'm gonna poke your eyes out. I'm gonna cut your dick off and make you suck it, you fucking asswipe."

Davai Lama crackles sweetly over the common channel.

I'm cranking the pedals. The drones show up every time the rain lets up. I turn on the jammer and exchange the batteries for the cameras and other equipment before getting back on the bike. A quick check on Warvid.Zone reveals no broadcasts or new videos from the territory of the plant.

Water drips all over the room, forming puddles on the floor. I lay the door across two planks, turning it into a makeshift bed.

Warriors in books and movies can fall asleep in three seconds. I don't know how to do that. I've tried a whole slew of breathing techniques and found one that sort of works when it's really needed. Nonetheless, I don't like to doze off instantly. The time before going to bed and falling asleep is the most precious part of my day. I first think about what's necessary, then—what I want.

....

1 Package 300—designates a wounded soldier in Russian military nomenclature.

2 A quote by Mark Twain.

[34]

[Hello, Atari]

"You've had quite a day, based on your pulse logs?"

"So-so. The staff at my resort are quite annoying today, but don't ask for details. I'm holding up OK for now. Better tell me about your day."

"I'm testing v 2.0 alpha version of your hand. Almost all the enhancements you're flooding us with are implemented."

"Can you show me?"

"Yeah… Can you see it?"

"Looks like the old one."

"You wanted it to be styled up with Hello Kitty[1]?"

"When you buy a new phone, don't you try to figure out how it differs from the old one?"

"We could come up with a new tattoo."

"Awesome, I'd like some silly Coelho quote from *The Alchemist*[2]. I want everyone to think I'm a very deep and spiritual person."

"Wait, what? You don't want my face or at least ♥ATARI?"

"I do, just not on any body part that can be replaced easily."

"How sweet."

"Um, can you shift the hand's control to me?"

"I can. Hold on."

Atari positions her phone stand next to the hand. I can see both the hand and Atari typing code on the computer. So beautiful, yet so distant.

She turns.

---

1   Hello Kitty is a fictional character created by the Japanese company Sanrio.

2   Paulo Coelho's novel *The Alchemist*.

"Try it."

I flex my left hand and see v 2.0 mirror it perfectly.

"Come closer, please."

I take her hand in mine, feeling the touch and warmth. We inter-lock fingers. I hunger to touch her smiling face.

"Hey… the walls here are literally glass. I think I can hear my colleagues giggling."

"Then stay late."

"Just go to sleep already."

Right, like I could possibly sleep now.

For once, I'm being roused from sleep by something other than just another danger alarm (I have the spectrum analyzer set to non-disturb mode—it should automatically turn the jammer on as needed).

A water droplet that has been forming on the ceiling finally breaks free and splatters onto my forehead.

Upon waking, I often experience a kind of eureka moment, especially when I have been intensely contemplating a problem just before falling asleep. It might seem like the solution arrives in a split second—as I open my eyes. The reality is that the brain continues to work even during sleep. When I wake up, it presents a question:

"What happens when a droplet detaches from the ceiling and starts falling?"

"Its potential energy is converted to kinetic energy."

Duh!

It's getting lighter—time to do some recon.

[36]

Keeping well below windows I run across the sky bridge, which connects my building to the production facility. It's an enormous single space twenty meters wide and sixty meters long. The multi-leveled roof is forty meters on its highest end. Most of the equipment that used to be housed here is gone. Only a few pieces of obscure machinery remain.

A metal staircase on the southern wall leads to the top. Halfway up, there's a 5x2.5m room with a couple of windows overlooking the expansive interior and a small one facing outside. This must have been a shift manager's office. It still contains a desk, a broken chair, and a few button panels with inscriptions in Russian. "Lunch", says one of them.

At the start of the war, there was a story going around: an orc squad was marching along a road through the fields. The leader noticed a doorbell nailed to a birch tree on the roadside. He laughed as he pressed the button. Only three of the twelve-person unit survived when a chain of ground mines detonated. Almost half of those who hear this story say they would have done the same. It's some kind of WTF instinct.

I skip the button—I can make my own lunch.

I scale the staircase (forty meters is the same as a fucking twelve-story building). At the very top, a gaping hole opens to the outside, where a sloping shaft connects the factory to a smaller building about a hundred meters away. It once housed a conveyor belt that carried raw coal upward. The rocks would be dropped through a series of filters of varying diameters to separate the impurities.

From the shaft, only the suspended carcass and a metal conveyor belt resembling tank treads remain. Almost all of the outer shell has peeled off.

A square opening in the ceiling serves as the source of a waterfall. The roof itself is flat, surrounded by a half-meter parapet, allowing me to crawl around freely without worrying about being seen from the nearby waste hills. The ground is riddled with deep puddles that make getting around quite unpleasant, even in my insulated clothing—water always finds its way in. Yet, it almost makes me happy.

I locate the rain drain, which is completely clogged, causing water to escape through the roof hatch. I remove the larger pieces of debris, then plunge my hand straight into the muck and start pulling out a concoction of dirt, leaves, and other junk. Bubbles begin to appear at the surface, turning into a whirlpool when I manage to dislodge a stuck brick. The small pool I'm lying in starts to drain. I cover the newly liberated waterway with a square sheet of linoleum ripped from the floor of the shift manager's office, then weigh it down with a brick.

On my way back downstairs, I inspect the downspout. It's made of thick metal and looks to be in decent condition.

Math time: I measure the area of the highest part of the roof:

`30 x 20 = 600 square meters`

According to the weather forecast, it's currently raining heavily—8 mm/h. Visual observation confirms about the same rate. This means that each square meter collects approximately eight liters of rainwater per hour. In total:

`600 x 8 = 4.8 tonnes`

4.8 tonnes of water at 40 meters altitude.

Fuck it. Too much math for my brain.

ChatGPT has been known to go off track with calculations, but I ask it nevertheless:

I have 4.8 tonnes of water elevated to 40 meters. How much can I charge with that energy using 40Ah 22V batteries?

I skim through the lengthy explanations and formulas straight to the answer: 55%.

If I could squeeze out at least 10% efficiency, I would be able to top up half of my batteries in ten hours.

At the bottom, the pipe disappears into the ground. It's unclear where it leads—possibly to a reservoir of some kind. I use a marker filled with acid to draw two horizontal lines around it: one near the floor and the other about half a meter higher. I find a short log with a roughly matching diameter and work on sharpening one end with my knife. By the time I'm done, the acid has eaten through the metal. A slight kick sends the section of the pipe flying off. I use a brick to hammer the makeshift plug in.

I return to the administrative building to collect all of my gear. The only thing I leave behind is the jammer—taking it would shift the boundaries of its zone of effect, and the russkies would figure out where I've moved. I hook it up to a fully charged double battery since I don't plan on coming back here frequently.

I head back to the pipe with the bike and the rest of my belongings in tow.

I fill a garbage bag with a mix of gravel and coal waste.

Hauling twenty kilos up twelve stories is no joke. Where's a lift operator when you need one? There's an elevator here—more like an open platform for transporting heavy loads—though even all of my batteries combined wouldn't be enough to power its engine, not to mention I'd need an alternating current. On the way up, I stop by the office to grab a few more linoleum squares.

The first thing I do on the roof is set up cameras: one for each side, except for the east. That direction is covered by a camera in the office window. I then deploy a Starlink antenna.

To complete my rooftop project, I resort to a children's game: building mini dams. The hatch opening is framed by a barrier. There's a gaping hole at one of its edges, forming the brink of a waterfall. I block it with a garbage bag and use other random junk—linoleum, bricks, and boards—to seal smaller fissures. Where is all the rooftop crap coming from? What kind of whacko eagles bring it?

Before long, the results of my labor begin to show: the puddles grow larger and start to merge. I reopen the drain.

Back downstairs, I knock on the pipe—it doesn't sound empty anymore.

Using the acid marker, I draw a small circle with a diameter of four centimeters just above the plugged end.

Soon, the water bursts through the acid-etched hole. I seal it up again by wrapping duct tape around the pipe repeatedly.

It takes an additional trip to the administrative building to retrieve an armful of spent foam sealant cans—I knew they were there from my initial inspection.

I cut the cans in half—some of them are still half full, which would have been useful during repairs on the roof. I take the lower parts of the cans, flatten the cut ends, and firmly zip-tie them to the rim of the bike's rear wheel. That completes my twelve-blade water wheel. The rear fork is quite wide, allowing the blades to fit into the extra space nicely. The can bases are angled to catch the water; their surfaces are slightly arched inward, which will capture more energy than a flat blade would.

I prop the rear wheel up on a kickstand, then remove the duct tape seal from the pipe. The water jets out, hits the blades, and makes the wheel turn. I've just reinvented the ~~wheel~~ watermill.

40-60 watts. Not particularly great. I could say that you don't look a gift horse in the mouth, but this isn't exactly a gift, and besides—I hate proverbs. If the wattage level stands, I can top up all of my batteries in thirty hours. That is, if I barely use them during that time.

The rain is forecasted to last until six in the morning, which I welcome as good news—it works for my benefit and keeps enemy drones grounded.

For the rest of the day, whenever there's a brief let-up in the rain, enemy drones show up near the administrative building, forcing me to activate the jammer. If the rain pauses for too long, I have to plug the hydroplant, as it's far more effective when the pipe is full. When the downpour returns, I pull out the plug and get back into energy business.

I allocate three hours for prepping my defences: mining and installing tripwires.

Time for a rest—I'm quite spent.

[37]

[Hello, Atari]

"When I was at university studying physics, our course had a few geniuses—all of them a bit crazy in one way or another. They seemed to speak a different language when talking to the lecturers. I used to listen and think that my mind would never work the same way. They would go on to invent and collect Nobel Prizes, while I wouldn't. That's why I quit. I don't see the same strangeness in you, even though it's clear that you're a brilliant scientist. Can you explain this?"

"Ha, my course had some of those, too. They wouldn't let me into their group, though. Did any of yours end up winning any Nobels?"

"Frankly, I don't even know what they're up to now. I would've probably found out if they did."

"Two of mine now work for me at Brainlink—I invited them myself. Sure their IQ is off the charts, but they seem to focus on a niche subject, ignoring the big picture. Inventions mostly come from those who know how to creatively fuse different fields. In America, businesses often specifically seek out dropouts. Anyways, you could've stayed and finished. Tell me, what did you do after dropping out?"

"I drifted around the world: Europe, Asia, Australia. I did photography, sold pictures to portals, freelanced as a programmer. By today's standards, I'd probably be considered a traveling influencer. One day, my Aussie girlfriend announced she had had enough and wanted to settle down. We tried—it didn't work out."

"And then?"

"I hitched a ride on a sailboat. An American couple was looking for an aide on a long trip from Sydney to Ecuador. We sailed for half a year, making long stops in the islands of Polynesia. In Ecuador, I bought a bike and set out on a ride around South America. It took another two years. I followed the west coast all the way down to the Tierra del Fuego and then traveled back up along the east coast."

"And it didn't get old?"

"I felt jumbled at times. Anyway, in French Guiana, I met a guy from Brazil who convinced me to sign up for the French Foreign Legion. We spent half a year training—he got tossed out, but I was accepted. I guess I was ready for order and routine."

"How long did you serve?"

"Six years. Afghanistan, Chad, Mali. I returned to Lithuania in 2014, determined to settle down. That's when the war in eastern Ukraine broke out. I've mostly been here since."

"Sounds like a Hundred Years' War."

"It certainly feels that way. But wait, I asked about you, yet I keep blabbering on about myself."

"My story is a bit more straightforward: university, followed by a string of engaging jobs. Married to a guy from the same course. That too went awry—he couldn't stomach the competition."

"Hordes of admirers?"

"Work. Ironically, as a little girl, I used to tell my parents: "When I grow up, I won't work—my husbands will work for me. I'll have many husbands.""

"Let me guess: the plan flopped?"

"Yeah."

[38]

"Davai Lama has found replacements for his losses—four fresh *pidars* are about to join your fanclub. There's no shortage of volunteers, and it doesn't look like the supply is going to dry out any time soon. He's got a lot of clout there—wouldn't let other groups join in—doesn't want to share the loot."

I read a message from Z3N3K. I need to clear out of here.

[39]
04:00 | October 2, 2028
Pivden, Ukraine

It's 4 a.m. Power banks are loaded to 58% capacity—not bad. The rain is supposed to stop in half an hour. That's when the drones will come to milk the jammer's batteries. I can hold out for quite a while longer, but is there any point?

This time, I'm not going to activate the jammer, allowing them to litter the admin building with mines. I'll wait for the assault unit to arrive, then slip out in the direction they came from while they're busy searching in the wrong spot.

Right on cue, the rain stops at 6 a.m. The generator runs for another half hour until the accumulated water is depleted. It's expected to be overcast without rain for the rest of the day.

A couple of drones show up, stop briefly at their usual spot, then tentatively approach the building. Not encountering any jamming, they get inside. Shortly after, two more drones arrive carrying mines. In just half an hour, all four manage to complete three rounds each.

I pack up the Starlink and cameras, replacing them with Magpie and Crow. I pop into the manager's office for my backpack and the remaining stuff—I spent the night here. With a heavy heart, I disassemble the watermill.

[40]

My plan didn't work, at least not fully.

They didn't just send one attack unit—all four of them are advancing in three-man groups toward my old building. Twelve meatheads in total.

Fuck the rules, huh? Each team is accompanied by a drone, controlled by a pilot left behind at the base, observing and reporting. The attackers advance slowly, with the leaders probing the ground for mines. They manage to find two—the extra effort is paying off in avoiding Dumdum's fate.

The northern threesome finally reach the building and clamber through its windows. No, those weren't mined. The other groups take positions to observe.

Worse still, there are no exits to the north—only to the south and east. The latter isn't even a true exit, just a massive entryway for trucks. Both of these directions are under constant surveillance by the eastern group.

[ЧІ]

Plan B. Keeping as quiet as possible, I climb the stairs again—yes, all twelve floors. When I get back home, I'm definitely signing up for a bodybuilding contest, showcasing only my leg muscles.

About two thirds up, I hear a drone enter through the massive entryway on the far side. There's no point, or even a place, to hide—if they miss me, they'll surely spot the bike—so I fire up the jammer. The drone turns out to be one of the dumb types; it doesn't know how to backtrack. It rises all the way to the ceiling until its sensors tell it to stop, then slowly sinks back to the ground.

All the groups mobilize and advance towards different entrances to the factory.

I hunker down behind the engine block.

A minute later, a thunderous explosion rings out. The trio looking for me decided to use the skybridge from the admin building. I had mined it, obviously. To be honest, it should have been apparent even to a complete dunce, but their hunter's instinct trumped self-preservation. I can see in the video feed how a cloud of smoke and fire erupts from the windows. Moments later, the bridge fractures at the point of the blast and plummets down.

Minus three and a point of access.

Remarkably, a single attacker crawls out—his head bloody—and stumbles hurriedly in the direction of the southern group.

Correction: minus two and a half (200+200+300).

[42]

Half an hour goes by.

The southern group approaches the leftmost entrance—the one closest to me. The entryways aren't mined; there are too many, and ordnance is scarce. I watch as they stick a camera on a telescopic pole, exploring the interior. The first one slips in, takes cover behind a piece of equipment, and sweeps the area with his rifle. The other two dart in as well, then begin creeping toward my position, following the cover-and-move[1] principle.

They'd need to come right on top of the bike to see it, as it's concealed behind a coal filter well. I lie on the floor of the top landing, observing them through a rusted hole.

The lead finally spots the bike and raises his fist—a sign for everyone to stop. One of them retrieves a grappling hook. He's going to attempt to snag the bike and pull it in—there's no way such prized loot isn't booby-trapped.

It takes three casts for the hook to catch. Toppling the bike does nothing. Encouraged, they move closer.

At that moment, released from my platform, three items drop toward the russkies:

- A smoke grenade. I light it at the top, so it's fuming in full when it hits the ground.

- One of the elevator's engines. It's a strange machine—the motors are installed both at the bottom and the top. The bolts securing the latter were etched out by acid yesterday. On its way down, the engine is trailed by a metal elevator cable I had attached to it, with its other end tied to the bike's seat. The engine does what it was meant to do—lift stuff up—one last time. Both items traveling in different directions pass each other flawlessly—the bike comes through unscathed.

....

1   A military tactic where units alternate between moving and covering each other while advancing forward.

- An anti-personnel grenade, which I release at the moment the bike passes the falling motor.

As the engine hits the ground, the bike, propelled by inertia, rises slightly higher, momentarily stopping at the peak where I catch it mid-air. The sole purpose of the smoke grenade was to allow me to operate openly. I detach a loosened loop and pull the bike onto the landing.

The grenade detonates. Thick smoke obscures my view of the results, but the screams from below attest to the damage done. Either the explosion or the falling motor accomplished its job.

[43]

The plan to escape via the shaft has a few weak points:

- I'll be a sitting duck while riding down the conveyor belt. The risk is almost negligible—the shaft is to the north, where there are no exits, and therefore is likely not covered. Nonetheless, I can't be certain there are no snipers.

- The shaft appears to be in such a shitty condition that I can't be sure it will hold both my weight and the bike's.

- I have no idea what awaits me at the bottom: it could be a five-meter pit or an enemy ambush.

The shaft held. There was no pit or ambush.

There was a fucking mine.

[44]

At a twenty-degree angle, the shaft extends for about a hundred meters. Barely braking, I successfully cover the hanging part, then, slowing down, I enter the building. The conveyor belt ends there, replaced by a floor of compressed coal dust.

A good place for a mine, I think to myself, but I don't brake. If I avoided all the spots I consider good for mining, I'd be left standing still.

I steer to the right, not wanting to go straight up the middle.

The blast wave sends me flying.

The most fascinating thing in moments like these is the speed of thought.

Normally, I think about things by speaking in my head. Brainlink has nothing to do with it—that's just how I've always done it, and most likely how everyone else does as well. This gives the impression of thinking at the speed of speech.

The following thoughts come to mind during my second-long flight:

- Fuck, I really knew it.
- The protectors on the lower frame should stop the shrapnel.
- Sharp pain in the right thigh—nope, some of it got through.
- If I'm lucky, I'll land on that cushy-looking coal pile, not plaster myself into the wall.
- I'm proposing to Atari when I get back home (WTF?!?).

Shit happens—I plant myself into the wall and black out.

[45]

The accelerometer registered insane momentum and a trauma-characteristic trajectory, then passed that data to the hand's computer. Acting like a considerate doctor, it began analyzing pulse, breathing, and about a hundred other parameters. It wouldn't have surprised me if it measured alcohol levels too—what if I got drunk and tumbled off the bike? A verdict was reached: the owner is not well; intervention is required.

The drug delivery module hammered in a shot of adrenaline. The defibrillator sent an impulse through electrodes attached to my chest.

I peel my eyes open. There's ringing in my head, my ears feel stuffed, and my vision is a blur.

I order a dose of modafinil.

The medicine kicks in, and my vision begins to come into focus. The left side of the visor is fractured, but the projection remains visible. The computer informs me that I was out for 33 seconds.

I'll get to the bottom of the engagement topic later—I need to take stock of the losses first.

I try to move my limbs—they're functioning. There's a finger-long gash in my thigh, but no excessive bleeding. Lucky—a tourniquet would be useless so far up the leg. As I don't have time for bandages, I order an injection of blood-clotting meds. The pain is being dulled by adrenaline; I can skip analgesics for now—there's quite a chemical cocktail circulating in my veins as it is.

The rifle lies on the ground nearby—looks intact. The bike, not so much. The front wheel is bent into the shape of Salvador's clock[1], and the panniers are strewn all over the place.

I ping the jammer: nothing. Starlink: nothing. I unfasten the backpack and slip out of it. There are two gaping holes in the bottom.

---

1   As featured in Salvador Dali's painting *The Persistence of Memory*.

I focus on the feeds from Crow and Magpie—they're still peacefully perched on the roof.

By now, the russians have surely figured out what happened.

There are three of them bunched around the factory's corner, where there's no direct line of sight from my refuge. The largest of them is energetically waving his arms—Davai Lama is delegating assignments.

I can see two more by the factory's entrance: one is propped up against the wall while the other is bandaging his head. I replay the recording at high speed. Only a single survivor has dragged himself out of the rubble after the explosion. He's now being treated by the fortunate survivor of the skybridge collapse. I presume the other two are beyond repair: 200 + 200 + 300.

The eastern group has fled west, behind the admin building. My guess is they're using it as cover while moving north, aiming to gain control of my truck entrance.

In total: six operational enemies.

I know what the group lurking behind the corner is waiting for: drone recon results. Oddly, I can't see any. My hearing's still super shitty, so even if they hummed up close, I'd only feel the wind from the propellers. The drones are likely back with their operators for a battery change.

I send Magpie airborne.

The western trio has already reached the corner of the admin building and has just stopped there. They don't have control of the truck gate yet. The most convenient observation spot—the northern base—is separated by a hundred meters of exposed field.

A bit afraid of open spaces, are we?

Magpie detects two approaching drones: one is coming from the north, and the other from the east.

How about we level the playing field? I get Crow flying, too.

The northern drone clearly intends to welcome itself through the gate.

Who invited *you*?

Magpie dives, aiming for the enemy drone. With just a few meters to go, it launches a carbon fiber net with weighted corners. The mesh spreads out, tangling the propellers. Minus one flyer.

I have more nets like these in my bike packs, but the time to reload is limited. With Crow keeping watch, I have to try. Magpie enters through the gate and lands nearby. The engines putter out, and their peerimrim-pim noise (oh nice, I can hear again) sounds a bit show-offy: Did you *see* that?

Crow's feed shows the eastern drone entering the shaft through its upper section—just above where it connects to the building— where the metal sheeting has come off.

I grasp the rifle and take aim. I need to wait for the drone to fully enter the room; the explosion has thrown me to the side, obscuring my view of the corridor.

The pilot is an idiot: the drone makes a slow entrance, giving me plenty of time to zero in. Bam—the second drone shatters into pieces. Warranty void, I'm afraid.

[46]

"You're trapped, Master-Shmaster. Gotcha good!"

Lama's voice oozes with smugness.

I know what's coming next: using the cover-and-move maneuver, they'll inch forward until they're close enough to daze me with a flashbang and capture me.

I wholeheartedly disagree with their plan.

Crow's feed confirms: the western group advances first. A single southerner, leaning around a corner, starts raining bullets at the sole window I can return fire from. Those zip by and slam into the wall above, showering me with shards of concrete. I don't like this.

[47]

If I were to count, the time I spent in various factories during the war in Ukraine would add up to several months. They're all alike, built to some GOST[1] standard. In each of them, power lines between the buildings run through spacious underground tunnels.

The engines that once moved the conveyor are missing. The wiring is gone too—most likely looted for its copper. However, the wall, blackened by coal dust, still features lighter lines. In the southwestern corner, the tracks veer downward and disappear into... a damn compressed coal waste.

I unclip the entrenching tool from the backpack.

The western window is very close. I stick the rifle out and squeeze off a few blind shots.

The bullet rain intensifies.

I start digging.

....

1 GOST—a denomination of state standards in Soviet nomenclature.

Crow's feed helps me keep tabs on the enemy—80 meters to go.

A slew of rapidly alternating activities turns into a blur.

...I shoot...

...dig...

60 meters.

...shoot...

...dig...

40 meters.

The shovel clunks against a metallic hatch.

...shoot...

30 meters.

...dig...

I wedge the shovel in and pry open the cover.

...shoot...empty the magazine...

I grab the backpack and Magpie.

Crow gets a command to land on the factory's roof.

I initiate the bike's self-destruction. In exactly one minute, a powerful shock will fry its electronics and detonate the remaining grenades.

...in through the hatch...

I catch a glimpse of a flashbang grenade arcing through the window.

I let the cover drop. Intense light penetrates the gaps, illuminating a confined tunnel. The sound of metal hitting concrete blends with a deafening BANG.

The water reaches up to my knees down here.

I switch on the night vision.

The tunnel terminates in a dead end here—the only way forward is to the south, toward the factory.

…running…

…counting steps…

…reloading…

50 steps.

The water soaks its way up the garments, making the wound burn.

I order an injection of antibiotics.

100 steps.

…the light behind me intensifies…

I look back to see them sliding down the ladder.

120 steps.

I reach a room with three exits.

Chased by bullets, I dive into the first one on the left.

I slow down—try running a hundred meters in knee-deep water. The number of steps suggests I'm under the factory. GPS, predictably, doesn't work underground. I zoom in on the satellite snapshot of the territory. At a fork, I take a right.

I go left at the next T-section. With each turn, I estimate my position, trying to keep moving in the general direction of the south.

I freeze and listen: no sign of the pursuers. It's unlikely they all got inside—the place is a maze with too many spots for an ambush.

I reach a dimly lit room. Light filters through an open manhole. I assume I'm near the workers' living quarters to the south.

I climb the ladder until I'm almost at the top, then wait for the GPS to acquire the satellites. It appears I'm beyond the bunkhouse, the southern base of the russians. For now, Crow stays grounded—I don't want to tip them off about me being back above ground.

I take the rifle camera I used for my sniper hunt and slowly poke it outside. The bunkhouse is fifteen meters to the north. There are quad bikes parked near its entrance, with no russkies in sight. I know for sure that this group's lookout is inside the building, likely holed up on the top floor, chasing a drone around and searching.

I stash the camera and take a few deep breaths.

I clamber out of the well...

...*run toward quads*...

...*unsheath the knife*...

...*arrive at the destination.*

I slash the tires of three bikes, then hot-wire the fourth.

Moving away from the bunkhouse, I hear a series of shots. Bullets are piercing the mud, chopping off grass tips. It seems the engine noise alerted the drone operator: We've been robbed!

As I swerve onto a narrow forest road, the firing stops. I speed along a tunnel formed by leaning tree branches. I'm convinced that if I reach the light at the end, I'll be safe. Thirty, twenty, ten meters to go. The light grows brighter as I cross the imaginary threshold. In my mind, I breathe out.

At that moment, the gas tank explodes under me.

[48]

The sky above me is the color of television, tuned to a dead channel. I'm a cyborg, which gives me the self-assigned right to use that phrase without crediting its author.

I need to get up, but I can't. My head is ringing, and my ears are muffled. A familiar emotion from childhood overwhelms me: my mother is doing her best to wake me up for school, but I'm desperately trying to hold out. If I just keep lying here, eyes shut, ignoring all her nudges, maybe everything will resolve itself somehow, and I'll be left alone to keep sleeping.

Someone switches the channel to the news. The mouth of an ugly-faced presenter is moving, but it's on mute. Suddenly, he steps back, raises his rifle, and fires. WTF? Are news anchors supposed to do that? I can hear the shots, but they're very distant.

A sharp jolt of pain pulls me back to reality. Davai Lama has stuck a scorching hot barrel of his rifle into the wound on my thigh. I let out a scream. My ears unclog.

"Look—the sewer rat has come to."

Lama seems genuinely happy.

"You thought we'd just leave our wheels like that—without a little Kinder Surprise, didn't you? Silly."

He turns to his buddies:

"Take everything off, search, and tie him up."

He steps on my right wrist while his colleague pins down my left one. They both point their rifles at me. The other two get to work. I note the time before the helmet is pulled off: I've been under for nearly four minutes. The drug delivery module is out of both adrenaline and modafinil—there was no time for a refill.

[Check defibrillator contacts]

The error message explains why the resuscitation system failed.

They strip me naked and zip-tie my hands and legs. Two of them fling me across the backseat of a quad like some sort of hunting trophy. They use a rope to secure me in place in case I try to slip off. Davai Lama is in the front seat, making a call on a sat phone.

"Yeah, we got that shithead. Be there in thirty."

Atari was feeling frustrated. It seemed she had hit a dead end. For a while now, the Brainlink team—she and her colleagues—had been shifting their focus toward the next logical step: a technology to deliver images directly to the optic nerves. Feedback based solely on sound posed significant limitations. If they managed to transmit visual information, it wouldn't just be a breakthrough—it would change absolutely everything.

Obviously, nobody hoped for a quick solution to broadcasting high-resolution images directly to the eyes. That would require millions of electrodes, and such technology simply did not exist. Nonetheless, one has to start somewhere. The project's working prototype had 256 electrodes. If they could achieve the intended result, they would be able to form something akin to a running text line or primitive graphics. Still, that remained far off.

Brainlink's initial versions were successfully tested on primates. The apes simply got absorbed in primitive video games. Unfortunately, that wasn't a perfect test case for image transmission—you can't ask a chimp to describe what it sees. Human trials were a risky affair, especially after the lawsuits. Surgeons estimated that the operation to implant the electrodes posed a significant risk of permanent damage to the patients' vision. No thanks, said the volunteers. The only ones signing up were the sight-impaired who had nothing to lose. Still, Atari decided against deploying the technology in its current state until a significant breakthrough could be achieved.

Coincidentally, without any heads-up, Eaton barged into the laboratory today. He dropped by Atari to complain about the slow progress, suggesting that he might have to take over as the project's lead and show everyone how it's done. Just give me the implants and I'll find the willing patients, he said.

Having vented his frustration, he headed to meet Rajeev.

Rajeev was responsible for handling endless Master's requests for hand enhancements. Most of these requests were feasible—not rocket science. Master wanted a lockpick integrated into the index finger; removing the artificial skin would expose the tool, allowing him to pick virtually any lock. The middle finger would get an embedded camera beneath its nail, which would be useful for peeking around corners or surveying hard-to-reach places.

Eaton was childishly fascinated by those spy toys. He demanded a camera be installed in the ring finger, reserving the middle finger for himself—a mini flamethrower, to be precise. *I want it*, was his only argument. Obviously, his wish wasn't granted. Instead, the engineers installed a torch lighter that operates on compressed gas and produces a flame as hot as 1500°C[1].

Rajeev now stands in Atari's office. In his hand, he holds… a hand. The middle finger's artificial skin is mostly melted off with only a few drooping scraps remaining.

"We need a slightly more heat-resistant skin."

"Was *I* supposed to think about that? You were implementing a fucking flamethrower, not a watering can, after all."

Atari caught herself thinking about how annoying it was to say words out loud. All of them, not just the mean ones. Communicating through thoughts is so much more efficient.

Turns out, Eaton snatched the hand prototype from Rajeev, bent its fingers into a fuck gesture, and took off running around the lab, thrusting a flaming middle finger in everyone's faces until it ran out of gas. A fucking kindergarten.

Still, the main reason behind Atari's irritation and unease was something else: it had been a full day since Master's last contact. Moreover, he had been offline for most of it.

....
1   1500C = ~2700F.

I'm being transported. My legs and head are dangling on opposite sides of the bike. I close my eyes to shield them from the mud splattered by the wheels. It helps with motion sickness too—I don't want to feel nauseous. I realize that within roughly half an hour, in temperatures just above freezing, naked and wet, with the wind pleasantly refreshing me, I'll be between the first and second stages of hypothermia.

I will myself to stay positive. They let me keep my hand out of ignorance. You'd have to look very closely; the connection is disguised by dark tattoos stretching across the artificial wrist and the remaining arm. Evidently, they overlooked it.

Retaining the hand means I still have the drug delivery module. It's housed in the space within the connection, linked to the live arm via a tube and a catheter. It's the first and probably the most important enhancement I asked Brainlink to implement.

I command that all feedback be switched to voice—there's no screen in front of me anymore. I request a report on the remaining drugs:

- Adrenaline: 0%

- Modafinil: 0%

- Antibiotics: 50% (single dose)

- Blood clotting agent: 50% (single dose)

- Steroid anti-inflammatories: 100% (2 doses)

- Analgesics: 100% (2 doses)

- Opioid analgesics: 100%

I need to make use of these while I still can. I order an injection of antibiotics, anti-inflammatories, and two doses of regular analgesics. The latter should help keep the shivering in check, which is about to kick in and become uncontrollable. I avoid opioids for now—there's no need. The full dose is my ticket to the other side, should I see no other way out.

As the drugs start to take effect, I try to dismiss thoughts of being cold. Since I can't quite manage to think about anything else, I need a mantra:

"I'm not cold."

My brain pulls a fast one on me and responds with a poem:

> … *I'm really not cold,*
> *Though this morning was quite frigid and bold.*
> *I walk with my coat unbuttoned wide,*
> *So everyone can see my red scarf[1] and my pride.*

Whaaaat??? Why did this soviet crap have to drift up now? I believe I was in fourth grade when I recited this—still wearing that red rag around my neck—and I hadn't thought about it at all in the past forty years.

I make a sudden mental jump to 11th grade. We were supposed to memorize at least a page of *Hamlet* for today's literature class. The teacher is calling each student alphabetically, starting from the end. It makes no difference to me—my surname starts with an M, which conveniently sits in the middle of the list. I'm not quite sure why she always has to start either from the beginning or the end—never from the middle. Hamlet drills aside, she's an excellent teacher, especially when it comes to reflecting on life's subjects.

I wasn't prepared, as usual. All my hopes are pinned on the bell. I'm trying to learn it while others are reciting, but it's not looking good. I can name a hundred Pi decimals and remember all the significant—and not necessarily historical—dates, but poetry just isn't for me. There's no logic or numbers in it. I know the answers to all its questions. *To be or not to be?*—To be. *Or to take arms against a sea of troubles?*—Take.

A few slackers admit their blunder. There's only one girl left standing between me and arrows and projectiles of cruel fate.

....

1   The red scarf is a neckerchief worn by members of the (mandatory) "young pioneers" organization in the Soviet Union, and some other countries of the soviet block.

Monika, whom all the guys would fall in love with at some point, steps in front of the class, breathes in, and begins.

With all hopeless efforts already abandoned, I watch her (yes, just as lovestruck as everyone else) and await the inevitable. Except she doesn't stop at one page. She recites ten and would probably continue if it weren't for the bell. Thank you, Monika. Also, seriously?!?

An engine sputtering out drags me back to reality. It's cold, but I'm certain I haven't progressed to the second stage of hypothermia. Thanks again, Monika.

[51]

I tilt my head up and force one eye open—my face is plastered with layers of mud. Next to a russian medevac[1], four people in military uniforms are fidgeting in place. One, wearing a red plus sign on an armband, resembles a sad donkey.

I get dumped in a puddle at their feet.

"Here's your beauty queen. I'll need a written receipt for the delivery of this animal."

A kick connects. I curl up into a ball—head next to knees. While his receipt slip is being made out, Lama is eagerly having a conversation with me: plants kicks to exposed areas followed by sweet words.

"Hey, Master, I was told…"

Kick to my back…

"Professor will gut you…"

…to the neck…

"Examine what's there inside you…"

…to the ass…

"While keeping you alive. He'll chop off one leg…"

…to the leg…

"Then he'll apply a tourniquet."

…to the knee…

"Next, he'll cut your other leg off…"

The kicking pauses. The puddle water has softened the mud caked on my face—I manage to open both eyes. Lama is standing nearby, his lips moving as he reads.

"Alright, let's swap."

---

1 Medevac—refers to a specialized vehicle or aircraft used for evacuation of injured soldiers from the battlefield to a medical facility.

He stuffs the note into his pants pocket and heads toward his quad. After a few steps, he stops, turns back, and squats beside me.

"You know, I envy him so much. I mean, Professor."

He stabs a knife deep into my thigh.

"Please excuse me—I just couldn't help it."

[52]

I don't scream. Not because I'm a badass—there's a dose of analgesics circulating in my bloodstream that's large enough to knock out a horse.

I'm being transported again. It's significantly warmer inside the medevac. A medic, likely responsible for ensuring I reach my destination alive, is examining the wound that Lama inflicted. It's bleeding, but not in a volume that would indicate arterial damage.

"Not critical."

He rummages through his bag and retrieves a roll of bandages. Wrapping gauze around legs that are tied is quite a complicated task.

"Untie his legs… Wait, not yet."

He fishes out a vial and a syringe, snaps the top off, and draws the liquid.

"I'll knock him out, just in case."

He doesn't bother looking for a vein—they're constricted from the cold—he simply stabs the syringe into my neck and injects its contents.

I can still hear voices and smell disinfectant for a while; then, the next moment…

I'm eleven and a patient at a hospital. I was complaining about feeling dizzy, so they checked me in to run some tests. Frankly,

I'm not sure if the dizziness is real, or just an attempt to avoid the school. There are eight kids in the room: one other Lithuanian and six russians. Most of them are old-timers who've been here for a whole month or longer. They know a hundred tricks for duping the nurses: how to warm up a thermometer, avoid taking pills, or unswallow the tube—which needs to stay in for two hours—and clench it in their teeth without anyone noticing. They obviously prefer being at the hospital to being at home.

Sergey—or Seryi—is the leader of the pack. Before sleep, he reads books about the glorious campaigns of the red army aloud. Needless to say, his grandpa fought and slayed fascists with his own bare hands[1].

Still, Seryi's favorite hobby is harassing newcomers. He engages in this activity with double the enthusiasm if the new kid is Lithuanian. The kid doesn't lack creativity either: he fills slippers with porridge, rolls up a magazine into a tube, places it next to the ear of someone sleeping, then lets out a scream so loud that the victim is effectively deaf for half a day. Or, when the opportunity presents itself, he shoves the pills he didn't swallow right into your porridge.

On day five, returning from a routine test, I find everyone in the room having lunch. Today's menu features an exceptionally disgusting gruel. I suspect it's made from leftovers—maybe from yesterday, the day before, or even the whole week.

Everyone is quiet. Too quiet. Heads down, the kids are busy dipping their spoons into the slop. Seryi has already finished his. He gazes at me, smiling.

"You barely made it—so yummy today—I was about to eat yours."

I can hear a suppressed giggle. My plate is still full. If I ignore it, a nurse will come, yell at me, and make me eat it while she watches. There's no sink in the room, the windows don't open, and carrying it to a bathroom at the end of the hall without being noticed is impossible. The tactic of accidentally spilling it has already been proven ineffective—you just get more. Still, there's absolutely no

1 A stereotypical bragging phrase among soviet army veterans of WW2.

way I'm eating that; they definitely mixed something in.

I sit down on my bed.

"C'mon, eat it—it's delicious—trust me."

Warmth seeping through the blanket startles me. I jump up and pull back the corner of the blanket: Seryi dumped his soup there.

"Nurse, Martynas has soiled himself!"

He's howling with laughter while the others are cracking up too.

The texture of the gruel indeed resembles diarrhea.

Stepping quickly, I walk up to Seryi, who barely has time to slide off his bed. I clench my fists and get into position.

"One on one."

I say.

The smirk now gone, he nervously peeks at his minions, who are not eager to assist.

Catching an incoming kick and then pushing the leg up is an element of street brawling that my father taught me. I just put it into action for the first time. Seryi tumbles backward and slams into a glass partition that separates two rooms. It fractures but does not shatter. Now sitting on the floor, Seryi probes his head and stares at his bloodied fingers.

I spend the rest of the day in the doctor's office. Naturally, they yelled at me. When my mother arrived after work, they yelled at her, too. How dare I beat up a poor child whose father is in jail while he's being raised by a single mother?

By mutual agreement, they discharged me that very same evening. The dizziness went away by itself.

[53]

A falling sensation wakes me up. My muscles tense, but I can't move my arms or legs. The distinctive noise reveals I'm in an elevator, lying down, strapped to a gurney and covered with a blanket. Next to me stands the acquaintance from the medevac, while on the other side is a stranger in a white lab coat.

"Look, the sleeping beauty is awake. He was out for half a day."

The elevator doors open. I'm being wheeled through a hallway of a tastelessly decorated luxury hotel. One-third of the lower part of the walls is adorned with ornamental woodwork, while the upper sections are covered in intricately patterned wallpaper. The wheels glide smoothly over the carpeted floor. Even the ceiling lights feature some kind of crystal-studded decorations dangling from them.

The signs on the bulky doors set within baroque-style frames reveal that we're not in a hotel after all:

Laboratory #3

Laboratory #2

Morgue

We pass the morgue and stop at the next door.

Laboratory #1
Professor D. D. Pavlov
Authorized Personnel Only

The professor. I presume he's the one who, according to Lama, is supposed to chop me up. Whitecoat unlocks the door. Somehow, I doubt he's *the* Professor—he looks way too young. I designate him as a lab aide. He rolls me inside but keeps the lights off. I can hear keys rattle and hinges squeak. He pushes me—still on the gurney—into a cage.

The battle medic motions at my hands with a pistol:

"Handcuff him."

The lab aide cuffs my left hand then snips off the zip tie that was holding it secured to the gurney. He goes through the same motions for my right hand.

"Now legs."

As my legs are freed, he points a gun at my face.

"No funny business."

I can feel the blood rushing back to my numbed feet.

"Climb down."

I ease my legs down and slowly stand up. A sharp pain in my thigh reminds me that Lama's knife has been there. I feel so unstable and wobbly that I have to grab onto the cold bars of the cage.

The lab aide wheels the gurney out and locks the door. The medic holsters his pistol and drops a blanket on the floor—just barely within my reach. He pulls out a plastic water bottle and tosses it between the bars.

"You can relax for now. Professor will arrive only tomorrow morning—straight from Moscow. He had an audience with the president today."

Both of them leave, and I can hear the door being locked.

The only illumination in the room comes from the standby lights of a few devices and the green digits of an electronic wall clock.

[22:18]

If I were to believe them, I have the whole night to myself.

I pull the blanket in, wrap myself in it, and settle on the floor. I take a few sips of water. My mouth is parched—I could easily down three bottles like this but leave half for later. I feel around my wounds: the stab area is bandaged, with a faint dark blood-stain at its center. The shrapnel wound is dressed too, covered with a wide gauze pad. With my fingertips, I can feel stitches beneath it. What a surprise—the little sad donkey must've read the Hippocratic Oath after all.

I'm shivering now. I inject the remaining anti-inflammatories to counter it. Time to get to work.

I was blacked out for half a day. They must've taken me deeper into russia by now. A scan of mobile frequencies reveals nothing—I might be underground. As a long shot, I check for Wi-Fi:

0 connections available

The eyes gradually adjust to the darkness. Between the device LEDs and the clock, there's just enough light to take in the room:

- An operating table—they'll treat me on it tomorrow;
- Medical equipment. Maybe an ultrasound?
- A desk with a chair behind it;
- Shelves packed full of something;
- A tiny couch;
- A door in the far wall. Judging by its direction, it leads to the morgue;
- No windows.

I command the valve to open, causing the pressure that holds the artificial hand in place to drop. I entwine my fingers and begin pulling back my left shoulder while pushing the locked palms forward. The hand yields and slips off. I remove the catheter tubing, collect some saliva in my mouth, and use it to moisten the metallic cuff. Pinching the detached limb between my knees, I grasp the cuff with my other hand and force it off.

Time to go for a walk.

[55]

My robot hand is quite self-sufficient and can go for a walk on its own. The batteries are at 63%, which is better than I could have hoped for.

I shove it between the bars and set it on the floor. Moving my fingers makes it crawl toward the objective—the desk. It bears no resemblance to Thing from *The Addams Family*, which could sprint while ignoring all laws of physics. Out of respect, I decide to call it Hand—with a capital H—at least for as long as we're not parts of the same body.

Luckily, I've had some practice with this. My favorite game for killing time is called *Fetch the Bullet*: I place a round in a hard-to-reach spot, then puzzle out how to get to it. If I succeed, I try again with my eyes closed, relying only on touch. By any measure, I'm no newbie at this; I might even be a world champion in this sport.

There's a monitor on the desk, facing away from me. Judging by its shape and button placement, it's an Apple desktop computer. Hand is heading there now. The floor is clean, varnished parquet, providing good traction.

I activate a small LED tucked under the pinky's nail and point it every which way, scanning for the best route.

The desk's legs—metallic pipes—are attached a bit farther from the edge, making it impossible to climb onto the tabletop even if I managed to scale them. The standard-issue wheeled office chair sits on a single center stump, so it won't do either.

Mac's brain is housed inside the monitor itself—there's no separate box tucked away under the desk. Why exactly did Professor need an Apple? Is he what, a designer? A PC box with all the wires sticking out of it would have made a perfect ladder to climb. Technically, there are a couple of cables running upwards, but they're threaded through a hole that's clearly too small.

There's a drawer box, but it opens in the opposite direction. No chance of pivoting it either—I'd need a point of leverage to move heavier objects. I crawl behind the box, raise my palm at the wrist, and try to feel for something like a handle by touch.

Found one. I'm stroking it to paint its mental image: a curved, likely metallic loop—essentially a ladder. The drawer won't budge when I try to open it—it's locked. I pull myself up, wedge my thumb into the handle, and twist my palm, trying to reach the next step with my ring and pinky fingers. I find and grab onto it, then repeat the process all over again.

I drop to the ground. Fuck.

Again.

I tumble down from the fourth drawer. Fuuuuuck!

Again.

I almost break into tears when I see the light poke above the desktop.

Then, I fall once more. Fuuuuuuuuuuuuuuuuuuuck!

Again.

Finally, I'm at the top.

I crawl to the monitor and try to swivel it so that I can see it. Disappointingly, the monitor is not overly impressed by my effort.

Apple monitors do not swivel. If you're a designer wanting to present the latest masterpiece to your boss, you can't simply push and adjust the screen's angle for a more pleasing viewing experience. You need to move the entire stand, which is not possible for me without a leverage point.

Nevertheless, I can't let my climbing effort go to waste. I reach for the power switch. The screen comes to life, illuminating the entire room. I can see everything much more clearly now.

Next to the keyboard and mouse rests a circular pad connected to the computer. Professor—a true Apple fanboy—has a wireless charger. I bet he owns the phone and the watch, too.

What else can be charged wirelessly? That's right—Hand. I can't let such an opportunity go to waste. Hand crawls over the pad and precisely settles onto it.

I wait. Every three minutes, I have to nudge the mouse, or the screen goes dark.

There's a good chance my plan to use the computer would fail anyway, even if I managed to swivel the monitor—most likely it's password-protected. But, as they say, hope is the mother of the fools caged. Is that a proverb or a saying? Who cares; both make me sick.

The master of this lab ensured his cage subjects wouldn't get bored—there's plenty of reading material available. Newspaper clippings cover a nearby wall about a meter away, just out of reach, so you can't rip them off. Yet, the headlines are remarkably similar:

- Prime Minister Vladimir Putin congratulated Ph.D. D. D. Pavlov on his fifty-year anniversary.

- President Vladimir Putin awarded a medal to Professor D. D. Pavlov for his contributions in...

- Prime Minister Vladimir Putin congratulated Ph.D. D. D. Pavlov on his sixty-year anniversary.

The collection continues with more of the same blah blah about awards and achievements.

The photos portray a steadily swelling russian fürer alongside a gradually balding, bearded, mustached, and bespectacled mid-dle-aged man. He oddly reminds me of Professor Preobrazhensky from *A Dog's Heart*[1].

The batteries are full, and I'm out of reading materials—time for new ideas.

To turn the monitor my way I need a leverage point. Or… a rope.

The wireless charger is connected to a USB-C port on the monitor. Its cable is about a meter long.

I grab the charging pad and hike to the edge of the desk. With my pinky, I hook onto the corner while using my thumb and index finger to pull the wire.

And yet it moves![2]

I rotate it just enough to see. At the center of the screen is a lonely circle with a head-shaped icon. Shit—no auto-login.

I crawl back to the mouse and aim the cursor at the circle.

A fucking password prompt pops up.

If I knew the name of Pavlov's dog (not this one, but the one that made canines salivate by ringing a bell), I'd try it first. But I don't.

I cast another glance at the newspaper clippings.

Professor hit fifty when putin was prime minister—between 2008 and 2012 (I wasn't lying when I said I was good with dates).

The sixty-year congratulations came between 2018 and 2022.

There's no clipping for the seventieth anniversary, yet the medic mentioned that Professor was due to return tomorrow (well, today, as it's past midnight) from Moscow, where he was meeting with the president.

Could he have gone there to be congratulated? It's 2028—it all adds up.

Professor's likely birthdate is October 2nd, 1958.

....

1   Novella *A Dog's Heart* by Mikhail Bulgakov.
2   A famous quote attributed to Galileo Galilei who tried to prove the heliocentric model of the solar system.

There's no guarantee that the czar met him on the exact day, but I can't verify it.

I push the keyboard all the way up to the monitor. After a few tries, I manage to prop it up so it stands vertically, allowing me to see the letters. I begin typing:

```
1958        - incorrect password
195810      - incorrect password
19581002    - incorrect password
5810        - incorrect password
581002      - incorrect password
1058        - incorrect password
021058      - incorrect password
pavlov58    - incorrect password
pavlov5810  - incorrect password
```

I know I'm stabbing in the dark—there are endless variations. I'm latched onto the birthdate because I have nothing else.

I have only one attempt left. If I get it wrong, the computer will lock up, and they'll know someone tried to log in.

In truth, there's another computer in the lab—an ultrasound (?) device complete with a monitor, keyboard, and mouse. Such an impersonal instrument shouldn't be password-protected.

I quickly whip up a plan: I'll drop the mouse off the desk and push it toward the cage, where I can reach and move it. This will keep the Mac's display awake, providing light. Hand will have to repeat its alpine expedition and climb onto the desktop with the keyboard...

As I plan the route for the climb, my gaze drifts upward. Right above the device, a framed cover of *Time* magazine hangs on the wall.

Person of the Year.
Vladimir Putin.
Tsar of The New Russia.

I type into the password prompt:

`putin`

I erase and type in again:

`Putin`

Never in my life could I have imagined that one day this name would bring me so much joy.

Person of the Year

TIME

Vladimir
Putin

Czar of
the New
Russia

First off, I pair my hand with the computer over Bluetooth. My brain is now its mouse and keyboard. I zoom in the view on the screen—my eyes are practically popping out from straining to see from a few meters away as it is. Next, I create a hotspot.

In the browser's address field, I type: www.iplocation.net.

Hmmm… It indicates I'm in Hong Kong. Bullshit. There's no VPN[1] running on the computer, which can only mean that the router it's connected to is getting its internet uplink through a VPN in the Special Administrative Region of China.

I ping Z3N3K. It's the middle of the night, but the reply comes back immediately—he's committed to his hacker of the night image. I lay out the situation to him.

"A Mac, you say? Give me a minute."

He sends me a link to a file, which I download and run on Professor's computer.

Without my input, the mouse cursor starts moving across the screen. Z3N3K is launching one program after another, opening files—doing his hacker stuff. The program I downloaded allows him to control the computer as if he were sitting here in person, in the chair behind the desk.

"Found ya. More or less. A few of the ports were being routed directly, bypassing the VPN—some services in Mordor are available only to locals."

"And?"

"You're in Gelendzhik. A seaside resort south of Novorossiysk."

I look it up on the map. It seems I wandered quite a distance. I can't rule out the possibility that I might have caught a flight while in dreamland too.

"Any reason why that name seems familiar?"

....
1   Virtual Private Network.

"Duh, khuylo's[1] infamous palace is there."

In 2020, A. Navalny's[2] investigative piece about Putin's palace by the Black Sea was published on YouTube. The territory, spanning 74 hectares, had everything in it.

There was a 17.7-square-meter classic Italian *palazzo*, complete with multiple pools, saunas, a casino, a spa, an aquatic disco, and a hookah-striptease room. The property also included a separate guest house-tearoom with an 80-meter-long footbridge stretching across a small canyon. Additionally, there was a russian orthodox church, an orangery, gardens adorned with classical sculptures, and even an underground hockey rink. Inside, the decor featured gold, marble, and one-of-a-kind furniture. The price of a single table or couch made by the finest Italian craftsmen was as high as a whole apartment in Moscow.

Ironically, the czar never had a chance to actually use the estate. At first, due to the incompetence of engineers or builders, the ventilation system didn't function properly, leading to the development of mold. Everything had to be torn down and redone.

In 2023-2024, Ukraine became crafty in sending fixed-wing drones loaded with explosives more than a thousand kilometers deep into russia. There were a few attempts to fly them all the way to the palace. One detonated nearby, causing no harm, but ensuring that the bunker-obsessed führer would never even think of setting foot on the property. Meanwhile, the defensive measures remained in place: the anti-drone jammer operated full-time, an anti-rocket system was installed, and the sea was patrolled by a warship.

....

1   putin's nickname in Ukraine: masterversion.net/putin (redirects to Wikipedia)

2   Alexei Navalny—a prominent russian opposition leader and vocal critic of putin's government. He died under mysterious circumstances while being jailed in russia.

Besides all the listed amenities and many others that weren't mentioned, the *palazzo's* basement housed a state-of-the-art hospital. The equipment and staff there could bring the master back from the dead—and then resurrect him a second time, should he die again.

I'm starting to suspect that I'm currently a patient at this hospital. I'll have to inquire if my health insurance covers dental—looks like a toothache just kicked in.

While Z3N3K is poking around the computer, I google about Professor. Or, more accurately, I yandex[1] him—there's more info there.

Dmitry Pavlov—the most prominent russian neuroscientist and neurosurgeon—putin's darling. I even find rumours about the dictator letting Professor take over his palace's hospital—he woudn't dare to go there himself anyway.

"Your professor is rather paranoid. Or maybe he's just—what's the word... vo... voyeuristic—Z3N3K informs me. He has access to the security system and can monitor and control all the cameras."

"Lots of security and personnel?"

"Haven't looked into that, yet. There's a shitload of cameras, tho."

"Let me know when you figure it out."

"Also, there's a fuckton of files on his 'puter, but it's all science shit, not for me."

"Hm, can you grant access to another IP[2]?"

"What kind of question is that?"

---

1 Yandex—a popular russian search engine.

2 An IP address—a unique number which identifies computers on the internet and other networks.

"See you, Paul."

Atari waves goodbye to a security guard.

"Have a good evening, Mrs. Hunter. Leaving early?"

"Even I need to rest once in a while."

Especially on the days when the boss visits, she adds to herself. A robotaxi is already waiting for her outside.

"Hello, Mrs. Atari. Your destination is…"

[Hello, Atari]

"Hi."

"Stop, cancel!"

"Eh?"

"Sorry, I was talking to another… robot."

"Should I be jealous?"

"Stay offline more often, and find out…"

"I'll tell you later. Do you happen to know Dmitry Pavlov?"

"I do. Member of the mad scientists club. Why?"

"I'm at his place. He graciously agreed to share his research. Want to take a look?"

[58]

Thank God for AI—and for the natural I, for that matter.

Professor's files took up nearly a terabyte. The majority of them were in russian. The folder structure was a complete mess: dates, numbers, *new folder*, etc.

Atari spun a new AI project and fed it the entire dataset. The artificial intelligence translated the documents, analyzed the semantics, and generated a vector database.

She could now pose questions in natural language, requesting summaries. Before the AI revolution, it would've taken weeks to retrieve anything useful from such an enormous amount of data.

One of the areas of Pavlov's research was longevity—the science of lifespan extension. It's not exactly neuroscience, but who's to argue? Professor wasn't interested in the full spectrum of anti-aging measures. Like a typical mad scientist, he was obsessed with the search for a magic elixir. He convinced himself he'd found an ingredient—mumio, beloved by folk medicine and shamans alike—an organic mineral tar found in mountains. Based on its reputation, mumio, or shilajit, was said to heal everything. Pavlov entertained ideas on how to amplify its effects multiple-fold. Good luck multiplying a zero.

As for neuroscience, he was interested in enabling autonomic brain function—without a body. This interest wasn't just theoretical; the summaries also mentioned practical experiments that had been carried out. The finest traditions of soviet science right there. As far back as Stalin's era, Ilya Ivanov attempted to develop a human-ape hybrid—a super soldier to help conquer the world. A bit later, Vladimir Demikhov sewed on a second head to a dog, not to mention the experimental mind-control weapons…

Obviously, the mad scientists' club did not exist in any official capacity. The community would jokingly appoint their colleagues, who, as a rule, were exceptionally bright but fixated on some *idée fixe*. The obsessed would ignore facts that argued against the feasibility of their ideas, or they would try to jump straight to point C, skipping B—or, in some cases, even A. What's the point of developing a technology for the brain to function without a body when the signal interface is still in its infancy?

Nevertheless, the AI summary stated that, in recent years, Pavlov had been concentrating specifically on reading brain signals.

Interesting.

Atari requested more details. After receiving the new summary, she opened the link to the related document…

Her jaw dropped.

The document was authored by… Atari Hunter. She was looking at a description of Brainlink, version two.

How? Who? Fucking Ctrl+Z, Undo!

Sweating in anger, she opened the file's folder. Her jaw dropped even further. All the files had familiar names. The folder contained years' worth of Brainlink know-how, starting from initial concepts and ending with detailed schematics.

She sorted the files by date. All of them had been created at the same time—a little over a year ago. Could it have been a one-off incident, like a break-in or a data leak?

If the intrusion had been detected, she would have known about it. If it went unnoticed, there would likely be newer material as well. A leak, then?

She skimmed the list once again. Some of the files designated as top-secret were accessible only to Atari and two of her course buddies—geniuses, the brains behind Brainlink. Could it be one of them? Highly unlikely—both were scientists to a fault, caring only about science, not money or fame.

On the other hand, we can check…

Top-secret documents were stored on a server that logged not only who made the changes and when, but also who accessed them. Obviously, there was a possibility that if it was the work of a hacker, he'd wipe their tracks clean. Nevertheless, she had to check.

Atari opened the log and looked up the date the files were created on Pavlov's computer.

You! Son of a bitch.

"The perimeter is thoroughly guarded: fences, cameras, sniper nests, active patrols. Within the territory itself: calm, but it's still early in the morning. A Buyan-class corvette is anchored a couple hundred meters from the shore. Your lab is on the second sub-basement level, directly beneath the main palace."

I receive a report from Z3N3K.

"Can you see me?"

"No, your apartment isn't being filmed. But I can see a heli landing as we speak."

"Is Professor getting an early jump on the day?"

I do my best to tidy up the desk: I move the monitor back to its original position, push back the keyboard, the mouse, and the charging pad.

"Most likely, it's Professor—he has disembarked and is being driven toward the palace."

Hand crawls to the edge of the desk and plops down onto the floor. No worries there—it's impact-resistant. It returns to the cage.

"Taking the elevator down."

I reattach the catheter and activate the pump, which sucks the hand back into place.

"Walking down the hallway."

I handcuff myself.

"10 meters."

Fuck, the monitor is still on.

[Power Off]

I hear a key turning in the lock. As the door opens, the monitor fades out. I'm offline again.

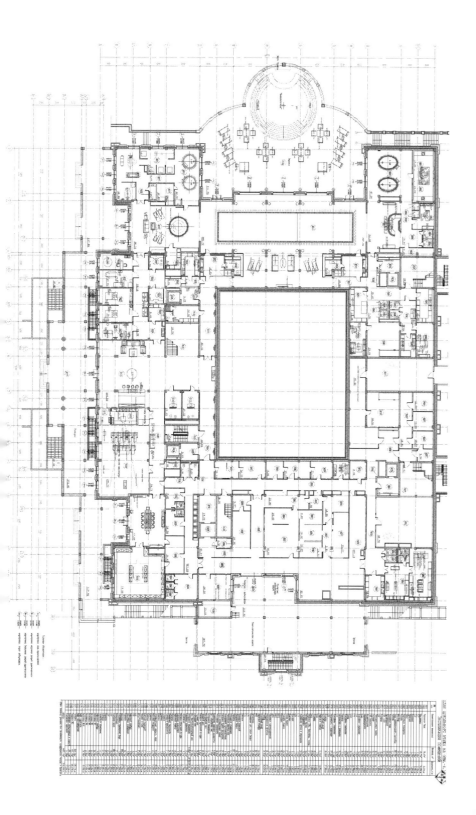

"I know about Pavlov."

Eaton tries to resist Atari's stare but quickly gives up.

"That was… ummm… a mistake."

"Really? Care to explain?"

"Remember when we got stuck with the first version of Brain-link? The health-impact lawsuits… The second version was just on paper back then. Pavlov got in touch with me, asking for the know-how and offering to conduct a lot of experiments and share the results in return. At the time, I was so fucking fed up with all the regulations. I admit—I acted impulsively."

"More like idiotically."

"Agreed. No harm done, though—russian shithands couldn't even build a working prototype. We already had V2 ready for deployment when Pavlov begged for a sample, saying he'd copy it and run all the promised tests…"

"And?"

"I refused. Like I said, it was a spontaneous act. I had a feeling where he'd get his experiment subjects—I know how the russians value life. I realized my guilt would consume me."

"Well, they got their hands on a sample."

"How?"

"They have Master."

"Good morning, good morning!"

Professor greeted me energetically as he entered the lab.

"How was the night? Rest well?"

Professor looked good for a 70-year-old. Still, he walked with a slight limp, and his hairline seemed to have seen better days—evidently, the magic elixir did not cure baldness (Atari was able to tell me about her findings just in time).

He tossed the keys and the hat covering his shiny dome onto the desk. Putting the briefcase down, he opened it, retrieved some kind of medal, and twirled it a bit between his fingers. Then, he slumped into the chair.

"Received this yesterday. From the president himself! For my accomplishments to the motherland. Congratulated me on my jubilee, too. Beautiful, isn't it?"

Professor clearly wasn't bothered that his patient stayed silent.

"But where are my manners? How tactless of me! You must be starving!"

He picked up the receiver from the stationary phone and pressed a button.

"Zina, prepare breakfast for our guest. For me as well. Yes, the usual. Thanks, you're amazing."

The medal obviously was the cause of his elated mood.

His hand reached to turn on the Mac but fell short—I had failed to move the computer back into its exact spot. He frowned and stood up to adjust the monitor but didn't power it on.

"I almost forgot, in all this joy..."

He limped hurriedly to the fridge by the far wall. Bottles filled with black liquid were lined up on its door shelf. He gulped down the contents of one.

"Delightful. Disgusting at first, but once you acquire a taste... I'd offer you some, but I doubt you'd like it. Besides, it takes a while for the effect to kick in—you'd need to use it consistently for a long time. I'm not entirely sure you have that long, ha ha!"

He approached the cage and gazed intently.

"How old did you say you were? Almost fifty? You look quite good, if a bit mangled. Found some magic elixir of your own, maybe?"

Giggling, he went back to the desk. As he reached out to turn on the Mac for the second time, a knock sounded at the door.

"Come in, Zinochka."

A curvy woman wheeled in a cart—just like in hotels—with breakfast laid out on it. She aligned it with the desk, wished a good day, and left. Professor grabbed one of the trays and exclaimed:

"And now, my favorite part!"

He fished a tiny bell out of a drawer and rang it expressively, then brought the tray to the cage and pushed it through an opening at the bottom of the door.

"There you go, dig in. You got that, right?"

He lingered, waiting for an answer, but didn't seem disappointed when there was none.

"I'm building a conditioned reflex in you! Just like my great-great-grandfather used to do with little dogs! Ha ha ha! If only there were enough time!"

Overly smug, he dug into his breakfast. That didn't stop him from talking, though.

"Eat, eat. You never know—this might be your last time. I'll grab a bite and be with you shortly. I was itching to get my hands on a working sample. How do I know, you ask? Well, do you know that Warvid is Eaton's project? He wouldn't tell anyone, but I do know, apparently! I've been waiting for a streamer with superpowers to show up. The first seven didn't work out, but from what I've heard about you, I'm sure my wait is over! Eighth time's the charm!"

The phone rang.

"Pavlov here. Who? Ahhhh! A pleasure. You have my eternal gratitude. Yes, we were just having breakfast and a discussion. No, he didn't mention you. Hmmm, how long would it take for you to get here? Well… fine, for you, I'll do my best. The back? Yoga doesn't help, you say? It's OK, Nastia happens to be spending her vacation here with us—she'll fix you right up. Good, see you soon. Alright, I'll pass it on."

He put the receiver down and broke into a grin:

"You'd never guess who just called! Your good pal Davai Lama! He sends his regards and asks not to rush with the expe… examination—says he'd love to be there for everything. I gave him my word to wait a bit—he's flying in. He also mentioned his back hurts after you almost blew him up. Why would you do something like that? Ha ha!"

There was another knock on the door.

"Come in!"

The already familiar whitecoat entered.

"Ah, it's you, Genady."

"Good morning, Professor."

"Let's delay the procedure a little—we're expecting guests. Davai Lama is flying in. I'm under the impression, you'd rather not step into that cage alone."

"Sure, I can wait."

"Good, good. I'll ring you when I need you. Listen, did you clear out the morgue? There's only one slot left in the freezer. As you can see, we already have a candidate. How does it go? A good place is never empty, ha ha!"

"They're taking all of them away today."

"Great, great. I'll call you."

Genady sighed with relief and bailed out.

Professor finished his breakfast, licked his fingers clean, and joyfully smacked his lips before finally turning on the computer. I hoped he'd shut up now, at least for a while. Unfortunately, this fucking bird considered silence unacceptable.

"Wow, so many well-wishers. Aw, thanks, thanks."

He checked his mail, rejoicing at every message, noting the ranks, names, surnames, and father's names[1], while reading the greetings aloud.

I tuned him out. A powered-up computer meant I had internet access—the hotspot launched automatically—and Z3N3K could get to hacking.

"Z3N3K?"

"Yeah, I'm here. What's the sitch?"

"The procedures were delayed a few hours. Lama is coming."

"Hm..."

"Hey, did you happen to find any clues if this disneyland has a self-destruction system? If I can't have it, then nobody will—BOOM!"

"I looked. If there is one, Professor does not have access to it."

"What about the anti-rocket setup?"

"Nothing. The katsaps[2] are too paranoid to keep it connected to the network."

---

1 In russian culture it's customary to address a person using their first name and their father's first name.

2 Katsap is a derogatory slang term used to refer to a person from russia in a demeaning way. Mostly used in countries like Ukraine, Lithuania, who were and are affected by russian agression.

Having finished reveling in the greetings, Professor cheerfully sprang up and drew closer to the cage.

"And what am I supposed to do now? Oh right, I barely got any sleep! Just a quick nap on the plane. I'm going to snooze for an hour or so, then come back refreshed and get to work in high spirits."

If he looks like a squirrel on meth in a hamster wheel when he's sleep-deprived, what will he look like when fully rested?

He picked up another bottle from the fridge, drew a few drops of liquid using the dropper built into the cap, and let it trickle into his mouth.

"For a better sleep. Exactly three drops for three to four hours. Would you like some, too? To make time fly faster—I know you're eager to start, haha!"

My silent prayer for him to pass out right there on the couch, not only leaving the computer on but also the keys on the desk, was ignored. He powered down the computer (What sort of habit is this? Is he trying to be energy-efficient or what?) and took the keys with him before yawning and taking off.

"See you soon! I'll keep the lights on—it's difficult to eat in the dark."

I haven't had anything to eat for almost a full day now—going on a hunger strike is not an option for me. If I pull off some magic trick to escape, I'll need all the energy I can get. And it's a king-worthy breakfast too: pancakes with red caviar and tea. Normally, I have my tea without sugar, but I add all five cubes this time.

Eating while handcuffed is awkward, but not impossible. What's impossible, though, is using wooden cutlery. Even as a child, I used to avoid ice cream on a stick. That wood-on-tongue feeling is nasty enough to induce convulsions. I dump all the caviar on the pancakes and eat with my hands.

My situation is fucked up, to put it mildly. That's why I asked Z3N3K about the self-destruct button. I could inject myself with a double dose of opioids while I still have my hand. It's a simple and, frankly, quite pleasant way out. Still, I'd prefer a more spectacular ending—one that would include a moderately sized BOOM.

I muse over sending the hand to turn on the computer, but reject the idea—it's too risky. I can't be certain that Genady won't drop in, or that Professor won't wake up earlier than he promised.

The feeling of fullness washes over me. Food is a very effective antidepressant. Everything will work itself out, one way or another.

I drift off.

[64]

Moments before plunging into sleep, it hits me—I know the solution, and it's so simple. I just have to get up, say—I'm outa here—and… just leave. Just like I did in the eighth grade after that fight with my parents.

A sleeping subconscious creates a strange mix between the present and that childhood episode: I'm riding a trolleybus in my dream. The route takes me through a quiet Vilnius neighborhood toward the outskirts of the city. All the passengers glare at me, knowing: he ran away from home. The trolleybus is being chased by russians on quad bikes. Yet, I'm not as afraid of them as I am of a conductor climbing aboard—I don't have a ticket, of course. She'd make me pay a fine, throw me out, and then—I'm done for. The pursuers don't get on at the stop because they don't have tickets either. I thoroughly scan the crowd waiting at the next stop—I know how to recognize the ticket collectors: they hold a slip of paper to pass to the driver as they board. I'd still get a chance to hop off through the rear door if I saw one.

We're nearing the last stop. I'm standing at the ready by the front door. The moment it opens, I jump out and take off running. Peering back, I see that the russkies are now pursuing me on foot for some reason. In fact, they're not russians anymore, but rather neighborhood bullies I constantly clash with. Pffft, those'll be easy to outrun.

I run for a long time, the pursuers long gone from view. I'm on a bike path that loosely follows the road, taking me further outside the city. A group of fighter jets flies by—they must be searching for me. I just have to reach the family cabin located in a small collective gardening community to be safe.

I don't have the keys, but I know how to open the kitchen window. It's cold and damp inside. I get the fireplace going and find some leftover honey to snack on. The sweetness overwhelms my mouth—I shouldn't have put so much sugar in the tea.

I push the armchair closer to the fireplace and doze off, wrapped in a blanket.

In the morning, the sound of a lock turning wakes me up. They have the keys, which means my parents are here. I've been found.

I'm disappointed. Instead of Mum and Dad, I get Pavlov and Lama, and I can't just get up and leave. Crap.

Lama seems genuinely happy, as if we're old buddies.

"Hey, Master, miss me much? I was so sad when they took you away. See, I even insisted they'd let me in here. Thanks to Professor and his heart of gold."

"Ha ha! Ladies claim I'm handsome, men say I'm smart, but I've never heard about my heart being golden before! With that, shall we begin?"

Professor unlocks the cage but lets Lama enter first. He yanks the blanket off, grabs the handcuffs by the chain, and lifts me upright. As soon as I'm on my feet, he lands a heavy right hook to my face, sending me bouncing into the cage bars before sliding back down to the floor. My vision darkens. A distant voice reaches me:

"Whoa, whoa! Easy! He's my unique specimen. Please don't break him."

"I'm sorry, Professor. Itchy hands. This should cut down on the wriggling, though."

He hoists me again, drags me to the operating table outside the cage, and lays me on it. The table has chain reels installed under each of its four corners. Each chain ends in a metal cuff that looks identical to slave shackles. Lama holds me pinned down—even though I have no intention of resisting—while Professor chains my left foot, then the right. He slightly reels in the chains to add tension, cuffs my right hand, and moves on to the left...

"Wait, wait. What do we have here?"

He leans in, examines it thoroughly, even pokes at it. He finds the connection line and inspects it, then brings his bespectacled nose closer and gives a tentative sniff.

"Hmm..."

He opens a drawer and retrieves a surgical scalpel. Firmly grasping the fingers, he glides the instrument across the tip of the thumb.

It doesn't hurt. The fingers don't even twitch. With just a second left, I disabled all the sensors and issued a command to stay still. There's a glimmer of hope that he might mistake it for a regular prosthetic.

Naturally, it doesn't bleed.

Professor makes a larger incision and pulls apart the artificial skin, revealing a finger made of metal, carbon fiber, and ceramics.

"Is he, like, some kind of robocop?"

Lama studies my hand, frowning.

"I think I just won the *Field of Miracles*[1]! An artificial hand, in addition to the chip in his head! Fantastic!"

"Does he have a fake leg, too?"

"Let's check!"

Professor uses the scalpel to prick the right palm and both feet. I wince as I feel the cuts begin to bleed.

"Nope. Bummer!"

"Check his dick, too—what if there's a pistol there?"

"Ha, you can check it yourself later."

He tightens the chains. The body is now strung up so tightly that I can actually hear the spinal segments popping as I struggle to breathe. I'm being quartered, just like in the Dark Ages.

"Look how firmly it's secured! No worries, we'll get it off."

Throughout the war, I always kept at least one grenade for myself. Getting captured by the russians is a much worse option than just

----

1   *The Field of Miracles* is a long-running russian knock off of the American TV show *Wheel of Fortune*.

going out quickly. Most soldiers choose to do it, as only a select few make it to prisoner exchanges; the rest are tortured to death, despite all the conventions. I was certain I'd be able to pull the pin when the moment came.

Well, that moment has come. I know they'll get the hand off me one way or another, taking away the option of checking out on my own terms. I shut my eyes and mentally recite the command for the lethal injection. The only thing left to do is articulate it.

I hear distant voices, but I make no effort to understand what they're saying. My brain is acting predictably, cycling random memories before my eyes. Those aren't even significant milestones, just a pile of personal *komorebi*[1]. The crunchy sounds of pine cones and small branches when I bike through a forest trail. How a warm drop of blood tickles my shin as it runs down from an old cut I just scratched open. The luminous algae in the moonlit Pacific. The shadows on the lake's sandy floor, cast by water striders disturbing the surface. I'd love to have names for each of those moments. Some serene Japanese words like *komorebi*. Or... Atari.

Nevertheless, the final *komorebi* takes me back to a significant moment—my first near-death experience. I'm about five, splashing around in a lake. I keep to shallow water since I still haven't learned to swim. The wind carries a small ball I'm playing with away, and I chase it, trying to catch it. The water is now up to my neck, but the ball is within reach now. I kick off, reach out, and grab it, but... the ground is gone. If I could get to the bottom, I'd be able to push myself up, but the air trapped in my lungs keeps me suspended mid-water. I can see sun rays breaking on the surface as a school of tiny fish swims by.

Dad's strong arm pulls me to the surface. *What took you so long?*—I complain after I'm done coughing up water—*I almost drowned.*

....
1 Komorebi (木漏れ日) is a Japanese word that refers to the effect of sunlight filtering through the leaves of trees.

I open my eyes. Back then—underwater—and in many other moments when I found myself in a tight spot, I never let myself think it was over—the end. I always somehow knew I was being protected. Going out by my own will—not for me.

Pavlov holds an instrument that resembles a dentist's drill, but instead of a drill bit, it's fitted with a small saw disc several centimeters in diameter. Bzzzzt, bzzzzt—he makes it spin a few times to showcase its functionality.

"So, what's it going to be: you give it to me, or I cut it off?"

"Cut it, cut it off!"

Lama can hardly contain himself.

I command the valve to open. Air rushes in with a hiss as the hand slips off on its own, pulled by the strained chain. The body, now attached by only three points, loosens up slightly. I can breathe normally again.

"Attaboy!"

Professor tinkers with the catheter for a moment before removing its needle. He picks up a small key hanging from the instrument panel and unlocks the cuff clasped around my detached limb. The chain and shackle slide off the table, clunking loudly to the floor. Clutching the hand below the wrist, he brings it close to the lamp.

"What a beauty!"

"So we're, like, not cutting anything?"

The cutting enthusiast is visibly disappointed.

"Patience. You'll have the opportunity to slice him up, just a bit later. I need to figure out how this thing works. I'll let you trim a limb or two if he doesn't cooperate, but I'd prefer to come to an agreement in a civilized manner. What if the shock from pain short-circuits his chip or makes him go coo-coo?"

"Shame..."

"You better go rest. Zinochka will feed you. Your back hurts, you said? I'll ask Nastya to take a look—she's a miracle worker. I'll call you if anything comes up."

"Well... fine."

[67]

Alone again, Professor plops down into the chair. He adjusts the monitor so it doesn't obscure his view of the operating table—he wants to be able to see his patient.

"Can you wiggle the fingers for me?"

I contemplate showing the middle finger, but that would just make him happy.

"No? Batteries empty?"

He retrieves a scalpel and some other surgical tools.

"I'm going to peel the skin off—it's blocking the view. It's not going to hurt, is it?"

I watch him work slowly and carefully, trying not to damage any important parts. He makes an incision along the length of the hand, all the way to the middle of the palm, then pulls the skin off like a rubber glove, turning it inside out.

"A masterpiece!"

He locates a magnifying glass in the drawer and leans in close, inspecting every joint, mumbling something under his breath.

Throughout human history, a severed limb posed no threat. It's dead. This concept is deeply ingrained in one's mind and is not easy to replace, even for such a peak genius like Professor.

The hand bends and twists at the wrist. It grabs the loose skin around the neck, pulls itself up, and clamps firmly around the throat. Professor's eyes bulge with terror as he tries to rip the hand off, but it's too late. Under normal circumstances, the fingers would exert the strength of a moderately strong person, but I activate a command that amplifies the force several times. I hear the trachea cracking, followed by rasping and gurgling sounds. Shortly, the noise stops. Professor's lobe slams into the keyboard.

Anastasia often caught herself thinking about killing her patient. Strangling this hunk of meat probably wouldn't work, but she could easily do it to that botoxed geezer. The only problem was that even during medical procedures, he was watched by two bodyguards.

Anastasia wholeheartedly hated russians, even though her passport said she was one herself.

But her surname, her name, and her heart all shouted: Ukrainian.

Her father, a miner, died in an explosion at a Donbass coal mine before she was born. Her mother moved to Moscow to live with relatives. She gave birth on March 11, 1985—the day Gorbatchov was nominated as the next secretary general of the communist party. The mother cared for her daughter only until she was five, before passing away from breast cancer. Nastya was left with an aunt she despised. The only thing she'd be able to lose herself in was the after-school ballet classes. The teacher noticed her talent and took her to see an old friend, the ballet superstar Maya, who eventually came to be a new mother to Nastya.

Anastasia had talent, ambition, and probably the best teacher imaginable, but her career was cut short at the age of seventeen when she shattered her ankle bones after an unsuccessful pirouette landing during a rehearsal. They could probably fix it now, but back then…

Maya sent her to the best rehabilitation clinic, where she became close friends with a physical therapist named Olga, who would give long and detailed descriptions of bones, muscles, and the processes that make the body tick. Anastasia was simply bedazzled. During the couple of months spent in the clinic, she learned more than she did at the institute of sport medicine she subsequently graduated from. She took a job as an assistant doctor at Moscow's Dinamo football club. Before long, she became a true star of her profession—injured athletes from all over the country were queuing up to see her.

One day, on her way home, Anastasia was confronted by brutes dressed in black, who showed their IDs, forced her into a Mercedes, and drove her to see... him. The same person she presently often daydreamed of killing. In fact, she hardly saw any other patients after that.

She naively hoped that fixing his aching back that first time would be the end of it. Unfortunately, the damn fossil would constantly injure himself trying to showcase his macho prowess. He'd dislocate his shoulder while showing off judo moves, or batter his ass while riding a horse or a bear.

They'd seek out Nastya wherever she was, even in the middle of the night, and take her to fix his problems. Those were becoming more and more frequent, and in 2015, they notified her that she would have to drop all other patients, stay close to the czar, and accompany him on all his travels.

Fed up, she tried to escape to her teacher-mom, who was spending her last days in Munich. The FSB[1] vehicles caught up with the plane as it was already taxiing for takeoff. From that day on, for the next fourteen years, she became a prisoner.

To be fair, she was being treated relatively well. But she was being guarded even better. Twice a year, they'd let her take a vacation, just not to a place she would have preferred. Her choice of holiday destinations was limited to one of the czar's residences. Meanwhile the czar himself was growing increasingly paranoid. All sessions were monitored by bodyguards, and she was thoroughly frisked before each procedure. They must've read her thoughts, or perhaps it was simply because her surname ended in -uk[2].

---

1   FSB is a principal security and intelligence agency in russia, a direct successor of the KGB.

2   A common ending of Ukrainian surnames.

The lump of flesh on her table was complaining about his back. A single stroke with her hand was all Nastya needed to detect the cramped muscles that were holding segments of his spine in an unnatural position. An easy fix, but she hesitated. The freak was bragging about him going to butcher some Lithuanian cunt afterwards. Nastya recalled warmly her time in Lithuania—the few summers she and Maya spent at her summer house in a hilly region among the lakes. She decided that she would fix the cramps at the end of the session, but it would not come cheap. Nastya jabbed her elbow into a sensitive nerve in his lower back and listened to the meatloaf's howl.

"Hang in there, it's part of the healing process."

With some effort, Hand drags itself out from under Professor's head, which is resting on the keyboard, then drops onto the floor and begins crawling. Movement is slow as its skinless fingers struggle to find traction on the surface.

The key that unlocks the cuffs is lying nearby on the keyboard panel. I'll be able to reach it once I reconnect my left limb.

I inspected the operating table while still in the cage. It's a large, modern model with a single stump leg at its center. Its vertical position can surely be adjusted, but I don't know where the controls are, and even if I did, I wouldn't be able to reach them.

And the main problem is that the leg is too thick for my hand to climb.

I look around as much as the chains allow me. Craning my neck backward, I roll my eyes, trying to see if there's any climbable structure at the head of the bed.

I can see the right arm extended upward, still cuffed to the chain that is attached to...

My brain replays the recent sound of the chain sliding down and the cuff thumping onto the floor.

I have a ladder.

Hand continues its march blindly, as I can't see it anymore—so close to the table. It reaches the base of the stump leg and circles its perimeter. It wanders for a while until I feel it touch something and hear a slight jingle, announcing that I've found the chain.

Climbing is relatively easy—I clutch the chain between my pinky and ring finger while reaching up and pulling myself with my thumb and index finger. I arrive at the reel and climb over it onto the table. Cold fingers pressed against my body, I insert the left stump into the artificial hand and activate the pump. It struggles to create enough vacuum—Professor must've damaged the seal when stripping off the skin. Still, it holds in place, which will have to do for now.

I extend my arm to grab the key, falling half a centimeter short.

I picture myself leaping towards a basketball hoop: as I aim to slam dunk, I accelerate and push up with my right leg, twisting my body to make it longer, knowing the ball is in my left hand. I rehearse it mentally and then just go for it.

I silently thank Professor and Lama for giving my tendons and joints such a thorough stretch.

[70]   15:20 | October 3, 2028

I unlock my right hand and free my feet. The body seems to bask in bliss. I'm definitely including more stretching exercises into my daily routine when I get back home—starting next week.

I have a bit of time, as it's only been half an hour since Lama left.

I power up the computer.

"Z3N3K?"

I'm disrobing Professor. He's significantly shorter, but I'm not a king and cannot wander around the palace naked. The secret behind his limp reveals itself—the deceased was missing a limb—his right leg is a prosthetic. Could this be the reason he is… was so obsessed with Brainlink?

The bottom of the pant leg is a good palm's width above the ankle.

"Wow, still alive! Sorry, I was sleeping."

"I'm getting out of here. You'll be my eyes and tell me where and when to go."

"Inside the territory—no problems. Just gardeners and janitors bouncing around. No idea how to slip past the perimeter, though."

"And the sea?"

159

"What about it? The wall extends a good twenty meters into the water. There are guards and cameras. Not to mention the mother-fucking warship is pretty close."

The jacket sleeves turn out to be similarly too short, leaving my robot hand shining in all its glory. I try to turn the skin right side out, but it fails. I thrust my hand into the jacket pocket, where it brushes against a phone.

"Hey, about that anti-air system. If I get it an internet connection, can you make it go boom?"

"I can try. It's a Pantsir-S2."

"So?"

"It runs on Windows, version 7, I think."

"You're kidding?"

"They showed it in one of their own propaganda flicks. It has some shitty interface all over it, but at one moment, you can clearly see the Start button, the clock, and the RU language indicator on the right."

The shoes are radically too small. Then again, I wouldn't wear those pointy monstrosities with golden buckles even if they fit—they're just not my style. I'd rather go barefoot.

I hold Professor's face up to his iPhone. It unlocks on the second try, once I force his left eye open. In settings, I set the automatic lock to *Never*. There's no connection down here, but it should come online once I'm out of the basement. I enable the hotspot.

I rummage through the briefcase and find a charger with a wire. Both ends are USB-C. If the computer runs Windows 7, it's too old to have a USB-C port. Wi-Fi is probably disabled due to security. I dump the contents of the briefcase onto the table, hoping to find an adapter for an older version of USB, but no luck. Fortunately, I find one in a spot where I would keep it myself—the top drawer.

"I have an iPhone with USB-C and USB connectors. Will that do?"

"Only if you find where to stick them."

I have to check something before leaving the lab, even though I already know what I'll find.

Behind the morgue door, I find a much cooler room. There are two wheeled metal tables and a wall with eight human-sized drawers. I pull out the first one. Then the second. The third...

Each contains a missing Ukrainian streamer—frozen, with their ears cut off and skulls opened.

Only the last one is still empty. It was meant for me.

I wheel a table back into the lab, heave the naked professor onto it, then push it back to the morgue and slide the body into the eighth drawer.

I don't have a logical explanation for what I just did. Maybe out of anger? Whether the lab is empty or contains Professor's body will probably make little difference to Lama if I'm not there.

I send a brief SITREP[1] to the commander of the streamers' legion. Mission accomplished. Time to bug out.

I check all the drawers and cabinets in the lab. A scalpel goes into each of the jacket's pockets. I find some duct tape and use it to seal the hand's connection, then deactivate the pump.

"Z3N3K, I'm ready."

"Not so fast. I've been reviewing a video of Professor on his way to the lab—some doors have biometric scanners."

"Finger or palm?"

"Palm."

"Left or right?"

"Right."

"OK, give me a few minutes."

----

1   Situation Report.

[71]

My artificial left hand clasps Professor's real right hand. A rubber glove is fitted over its wrist to keep it from dripping blood. The fingers are limp, with dark fluid showing through the rubber. I place it on the biometric scanner, and the door opens, letting me outside. I stash the ten-fingered thingy in Professor's briefcase.

Bright sunlight blinds me as warmth washes over my body. It feels like plus twenty-ish. I adjust Professor's hat and let it sink in—I'm at a resort. The distinctive smell of pines and sea iodine fills the air. The greenery is still in its full glory, with only a few trees starting to brown. A promenade adorned with exotic plants stretches into the distance. Fountains, columns, statues... I feel like I'm in a masterfully rendered 3D tour for an exclusive real estate.

The Pantsir-S2 is an anti-rocket defense system. It features twelve ground-to-air missiles and two 30mm machine guns, mounted on a four-axle Kamaz truck. Its sole purpose is to detect and neutralize airborne threats.

My hopes are riding on Z3N3K's hacking skills. I want him to launch those missiles. In the best-case scenario, he would hit both the palace and the warship, or, failing that, detonate the system itself. The ground-to-air missiles don't carry much destructive force—they explode a small charge near the target, unleashing a cloud of shrapnel that damages it. That won't exactly destroy the palace, but panic and chaos are guaranteed. It'll feel like a spit in the czar's face, too.

The Kamaz is positioned in the northern part of the territory, at its highest point, near the staff living quarters. The distance as the crow flies—700 meters; by road—double that.

I'm taking a ride to the Pantsir. Should I trek barefoot in grossly undersized clothes, or cruise in a golf cart? No-brainer.

I've studied the layout of the territory and know it by heart. Z3N3K is using the cameras to monitor me continuously, telling me when to stop and wait for a staff member to pass. After a couple of hundred meters, I reach an intersection where the road swerves left. On the right is an entrance to the underground hockey rink, while on the left towers a building of the russian orthodox church. Next to the arena is an enormous field containing two helipads, one of which is currently occupied. A person—a pilot?—is loitering next to the helicopter. He waves at me, and I wave back with my right hand. My left hand, dressed in a rubber glove, is holding the wheel. It's alright; anyone would greet with their right. The road continues among trees, painting a slightly skewed S-shape.

The Pantsir is positioned right at the top of the letter S, next to a tall communication tower and a short distance from the living quarters. Two questions are on my mind: Is the complex manned? And if not, how quickly can I break into it?

Could it be that they don't lock the doors up here? After all, it's a resort, protected by an impressive wall.

A positive answer to the first question makes the second one obsolete. While driving, I see a soldier reclining against the front wheel of the Kamaz, smoking. I drive further and park on the side of the road where he can't see me.

I get out and head toward the left side, practicing the stride of a confident person. The wounds on my thighs and the sharp rocks I must step on with my bare, slashed feet don't make it easy. I round the front of the vehicle. A short soldier sees a person in a suit and snaps to attention.

"Can I bum a smoke?"

A Central-Asian-looking face relaxes, the tension replaced by the condescending sympathy of a smoker towards a nicotine abstinent. He retrieves a pack from his pocket, flips it open, and offers it to me. I pop a cigarette into my mouth, while he extends a lit lighter. I lean into the flame, raising my left hand as if to shield it from the wind. I see the shock set in his face as he notices what the rubber glove and short sleeve fail to cover. At the same time, my right hand rises, doesn't stop, and, having built up enough momentum, slugs the generous soldier in his temple.

I'm kneeling in the control room of the Pantsir-S2, mounted over the second front axle, trying to unscrew a metallic plate that I assume covers the computer. An unconscious soldier lies on the floor, keeping me company, his limbs bound and his mouth taped shut. I was lucky to find a toolbox—unscrewing bolts with a scalpel would have been challenging. Two of the screws are flat, while the other two feature worn-down Phillips heads. An unparalleled quality.

I remove only the upper bolts, then wedge my fingers in and bend the plate down. Inside, there's a standard PC bolted to the floor. Two of its four USB ports are in use.

I hear grumbling—my roomy has come to and wants to get the party started. Just in time—I could use his help with the Windows password prompt on the screen.

I half-peel the gag tape. The soldier's stupefied eyes are riveted to the scalpel's blade, which I hold just centimeters from his right eyeball. He doesn't attempt to scream. Good boy.

"The password?"

"*spasibodeduzapobedu*[1], all lowercase."

Very original.

I reseal his mouth and enter the password, which takes me into Pantsir's control interface. Pressing *Win+M*, I return to the desktop. Using the USB adapter, I connect the iPhone, then type in the link Z3N3K gave me and install the downloaded file.

"Your turn, Z3N3K."

Z3N3K is silent, but I can see him working as the view on the screen constantly changes. Five minutes pass before my patience runs out.

"How's it going?"

---

1   *Spasibo dedu za pobedu*—thank you, grandpa, for the victory.

"Making progress, just need time."

"OK, I'll back off."

[73]

Z3N3K fiddled with the control software for a bit. It gave off vibes of something from the MS-DOS era—the UI[1] looked ancient. He found a window displaying radar information. Two green dots were moving across a circle, and the adjacent table showed two records:

```
| OBJECT          | COORDINATES    | ALT   | THR | ATK |
| civ.plane, RUS  | 44.595,37.925  | 7898  | 0   | X   |
| civ.plane, TUR  | 43.206,35.345  | 11245 | 1   | X   |
```

The coordinates were constantly changing and the altitude fluctuated by a few meters. A civilian aircraft from Turkey was deemed a threat, even if it was a passenger plane—it could crash on the czar's head after all. The X buttons in the last column were disabled. The checkbox at the bottom of the window indicated the automatic mode was on.

Z3N3K switched to manual mode. A confirmation window popped up: Are you sure? Yes. That activated the X buttons. A chill rippled through him at the thought that it was that simple to launch missiles at a passenger plane.

Another window was dedicated to the 30 mm machine guns. The camera was broadcasting the view in the direction the barrels were facing. It was in auto-mode as well. He switched it to manual and rotated the weapon by half a degree. The camera view shifted slightly. OK, all clear here.

....

1   User Interface.

167

The software was written in C++[1]. Any significant changes would require access to its source code.

Z3N3K checked the *Program Files* and found a *Pantsir-S* folder. He inspected its contents, then launched the task manager and glanced over the list of active processes. The radars were controlled by a separate program. In addition, the computer was running an Apache web server and a MySQL database. Z3N3K opened a browser and checked its history. The list contained just two addresses (no way for the guard to browse porn without an internet connection): a link entered by Master and a local web server address with a **/phpMyAdmin/** folder.

Z3N3K clicked on the latter. A login prompt popped up, pre-filled with… a saved password.

phpMyAdmin is a database administration tool, which meant Z3N3K now had access to all of the system's databases.

He opened a table named **objekty**. Its name was in russian—the first sign that whoever created this system was a moron.

The fields in the table were named in English. Where's the consistency, for fuck's sake?

```
id:                uuid
initial_date:      datetime
last_date:         datetime
threat_level:      tinyint
object_type:       enum
country:           string
```

The table contained a load of records. The ones that appeared on the screen were all of the same type—**civ.plane**. The second attribute of an idiot programmer: it should've been an **enum**, with the types listed in a separate table.

Z3N3K ran a query to list all of the records that weren't a **civ. plane**.

The visible results now contained only **helicopter**. Country of origin: **RUS**; threat level: **0**. These must've been how Professor and

....

1   A popular programming language.

the other guests were being hauled in and out. He rewrote the query to list all records that were neither civilian aircraft nor helicopters. Three entries appeared: **drone**, threat level: **3**.

He moved on to another table named **objekty_log**.

The table was enormous, containing the coordinates of every detected object, captured at one-second intervals.

Z3N3K wrote a query to insert a new record into **objekty** table:

```
object:         civ.plane
country:        RUS
initial_date:   2028-10-05 12:50:20
```

Once there record was in, he copied its unique id number and added a new entry to objekty_log:

```
object_id:      1226589
latitude:       44.30
longitude:      37.60
altitude:       10000
```

He went back to the UI that controlled the system and switched to the radar window. The circle contained a single dot—and it wasn't moving! The passenger planes from before were probably already out of the detection zone. The adjacent table contained a single row:

```
|civ.plane, RUS        | 44.300, 37.600 | 10000 |  0  |  X  |
```

The radar and missile control programs were using a database to exchange information!

Z3N3K opened a map. The missiles would arrive from... the east. The country could be North Korea—**PRK**[1]. Object type would be **missile** with a threat level of **128**—the highest number a **TINYINT** field can hold. He googled information about the speed properties of a supersonic missile and wrote a script to first insert a record into the **objekty** table, then add a new entry to **objekty_log** every second, simulating the missile's trajectory toward targets within the tsar's palace.

Friendly missiles had a table of their own, containing their

1   PRK—North Korean country code.

coordinates and altitude. Z3N3K's script would keep a close eye on these records, adjusting the coordinates and altitude of the virtual missiles to keep the real ones at a safe distance and prevent accidental detonation. The final destination for the virtual missiles: targets within the palace complex. Z3N3K's plan was to lure the real ones there.

Z3N3K looked through the rest of the tables. **no_atak_zone** contained a set of coordinates that, upon inspection, traced a virtual line one kilometer outside the palace grounds.

```
DELETE FROM no_atak_zone;
```

He emptied the table.

Now, only the fun part remained: choosing twelve targets.

74

"I'm ready."

"OK, give me a moment to clear out of this can."

"Fancy a prayer in the church? I didn't target it."

"It's russian orthodox; I'm catholic, kinda."

"Big fucking difference—same God anyway."

"I'm thinking about hitting the beach."

I'm cruising downhill in the golf cart toward the palace. I left Professor's phone behind in the Pantsir's cabin—Z3N3K requires internet. We're still in touch, though—there's 5G coverage, and the hand has a phone module with e-sims for all the russian cell operators. I backtrack by the same route I used to drive up. Without stopping at the palace, I continue south and park at a lookout built on the edge of a coastal slope.

"Fire."

"OK."

10, 20, 30 seconds pass. A mild disappointment creeps in. I'm starting to think the plan has failed.

At the 39th second, the sirens start to blare, followed by an announcement:

**Missile alert.
Everyone seek cover immediately.
This is not a drill.**

Sirens again. Announcement again. Z3N3K is a genius, after all.

Facing away from the sea, I look in the direction of the Pantsir. It's a kilometer away, in a beeline. One after another, twelve missiles take off from behind the treeline and head east, leaving white trails in the sky. I track them with my eyes until a telltale hiss reaches me after three seconds.

"Hey, Master, OK if I have some fun?"

"Come to my home."

"Huh?"

"Be my guest."

A clatter of machine gun fire reaches me. I can see the flames of an explosion somewhere halfway between me and the Pantsir.

"Minus one heli, he he."

Clatter again, followed by another explosion further to the north this time—Z3N3K certainly doesn't have a shortage of targets.

A dull bang reaches my ears, followed by a slightly different hiss. The sound isn't coming from the north, where Z3N3K is having his party, but from the sea. Turning, I see missiles launch in succession, vertically, from the corvette moored a couple of hundred meters away. Six of them—all much juicier.

"Master, you better hide."

"Yeah."

75

Davai Lama ran along a hallway—or was trying to, to be exact. That masseuse bitch didn't fix his back. Worse, she kneaded him in such a way that his left leg now barely functioned. Part of the healing process, my ass. Even worse, she made him wear that stupid-ass underwear. Can't work with your dick out in the open, she said. It looked like the thongs chicks wear, the ones with a string between their butt cheeks. How the fuck can they walk in those?

When he heard the siren go off, he instantly knew it had something to do with Master. Even if the threat was real, what place could be more secure than the palace underground? The czar had probably ordered a fuckton of concrete jammed in here so it could withstand even a motherfucking nuclear bomb. He leapt off the massage table and took off to lab No. 1 without wasting time getting dressed.

He rattled the door handle. Fucking locked. It gave way only after the third kick—the cocksucking door was made to withstand a nuclear blast, too.

Empty. Where the hell did he piss off to? Fuck, did they both get scared and went to hide? Lama checked the shitter, the morgue. He was about to head back when he noticed blood drops next to one drawer and opened it.

"Son of a bitch!!! I told you to fucking cut right away! That's what you get for not listening—got your own limb chopped off."

Lama went back to the lab to see if there was anything that could be used as a weapon. Nothing seemed to fit the bill. He ran back to the open morgue drawer and yanked off Professor's artificial leg.

"You're not gonna need it anymore."

Swearing, he limped toward the stairwell. That fucking masseuse.

The Pantsir system transmitted its radar data to the corvette. Either the ship's crew or an automated system assessed the threat as too severe—a level 128, after all—and launched its own arsenal designed to neutralize hypersonic missiles. I'm not sure what kind of ordnance those carry, but I'm certain about one thing: when they hit the ground, I want to be as far away or as deep underground as possible.

The palace's deepest point lies in its tunnels. One of them leads to a tasting room carved into the cliff, offering a prime sea view, as shown in Navalny's video. The second tunnel provides connection to the beach and the harbor. Both tunnels are accessible by either an elevator or a stairwell from within the main palace.

I sprint to the nearest entrance, beating all my personal bests despite being barefoot (the soldier from the Pantsir had an even smaller foot and refused to lend me his boots) and carrying Professor's hand. As it turns out, I don't need it anymore—the air threat alarm has automatically unlocked all the doors.

I know the approximate location of the stairwell from an earlier ascent from the lab. Though the palace layout is committed to my memory, I don't actually need it—the green, blinking evacuation lights guide me toward the entry.

I'm flying on the red carpets while russian czars frown at me from their gold-rimmed portraits. I must admit, carpet is a much better option than crushed rock or asphalt when you're going barefoot. The czars sense the danger approaching and want to escape together, but their short legs get in the way—or lack of legs, to be precise, since they're just portraits.

I open the door to the stairwell (being a model citizen, I always follow the fire marshal's recommendation not to use elevators in case of fire) and, taking a few steps per stride, cover the first, second, and third flights. I'm now between the first and second sub-levels of the underground. Grabbing the railing, I stop myself.

Standing in the doorway is my best friend, Davai Lama. He stares at me with a baffled expression.

I'm a bit speechless, too. It's not so much him being here that stumps me, but his choice of apparel. He's virtually naked, wearing only disposable massage underwear. He holds a leg in his hand, while I, dressed in the undersized Professor's suit, hold a hand.

"And where do you think you're going?"

Lama inquires, sounding rather polite.

An explosion rumbles. A string of explosions, to be exact.

Realistically, I didn't stand much of a chance. Can't say I don't know my way around a fight—I learned a lot while serving in the French Foreign Legion—but Lama isn't new to this either, and he's in a radically different weight class.

This is why I'm currently lying on the floor, lit by dim, blinking emergency lights. I can taste blood in my mouth that's missing two teeth. They were kicked loose by the Professor's prosthetic leg. I can't say I blame him, considering what I did—it's a fair trade. A few missing teeth can be fixed, but a much bigger problem is Lama's hands, strangling me.

Breathing becomes impossible. I can feel my pulse hammering, but I don't know how many beats per second, as the pressure monitor is inside the hand. Barely held in place by duct tape, it was ripped off. Lama didn't just remove it—he used it to batter everything—me, the stairs, the railings—until its fingers went flying and the palm came off. Then he discarded it and began strangling me.

On top of that, I can feel a dislocated left shoulder, possibly torn or at least severely strained tendons in my right ankle, an unknown number of broken ribs, and a mild concussion, at the very least. In short, I'm in mediocre condition.

Lama took some damage, too. I made surgical incisions in his stomach and hand while I still had a scalpel. He also got a facelift—a gash runs from his upper lip, across his cheek, splitting his ear roughly in half. He's just short of a matching cut on the other side to complete his makeover as the man who laughs[1]. That same wound is dripping blood onto my face. I doubt he's in any pain—adrenaline is a good analgesic.

I get the impression he's dragging this out—his gibbon-like fingers could easily crush my neck if he wanted to. He's clearly enjoying it. Words are coming out of his mouth, but I decide to tune him out.

....

1   *The Man Who Laughs* is a novel by Victor Hugo.

At least I destroyed the czar's palace. Judging by the tremors, felt even here deep underground, cosmetic repairs won't suffice.

My vision is fading. Through the fog, I see an angel with long, light hair appear somewhere behind Lama. He feels it too—hey, it's mine, you're not the one dying—and begins to turn. His grip slightly relaxes as I watch the angel make an abrupt swing with their hands.

Lama turns away and freezes for a second.

"Fucking masseuse..."

He gets up and plucks out the scalpel the female angel embedded in his shoulder. Too bad he turned at the last moment, and she missed his neck. The woman steps back, stumbles on a stair, and topples onto her back. Lama grabs her by the clothes and slaps her on the face with such force it could knock out ten angels.

"I'll deal with you later."

He comes back. The only thing I manage to do in the meantime is breathe. Lama considers such an activity optional and grabs me by the neck again. He doesn't even bother pinning my right hand with his knee.

With just a sliver of hope left, I grope for something. The fingers close around my robot hand, or what's left of it. I feel along the length of the catheter tube, ending with a short needle. Aiming for a thick, throbbing vein in Lama's neck, I jab the needle in. At the same moment, I command the drug delivery module to inject a dose of opioids—my unused quick exit grenade.

Bliss washes over the astonished face as his grip weakens, and I breathe in. With acceptance in his eyes, Lama stares into the distance.

"Now I know... Everything."

Lama's nirvana didn't last long. Grinning with his enlarged mouth, he collapsed, pinning me down again with his enlightened body. In fact, he might've actually been lighter—scientists claim the human soul weighs four grams.

I crawl from under the body, contemplating whether the soul's weight is proportional to the actual mass of its owner, or more to its depth. The process is slow—everything hurts. I should've saved a microdose of opium for myself. Or not—there's nothing to sterilize the needle with. I wouldn't want to use the one I stuck in Lama's neck—pain seems like the better option. My already swollen foot is the last to break free, but I remain on the floor for now. On my fours—or threes, to be exact—I crawl to my guardian angel, lying on the stairs. There's a pulse, and she's breathing. As carefully as possible, I move her to a flat landing, then lift her legs and place them on... Lama. More blood will flow to her brain that way. I ask loudly if she's alright and give her a gentle shake.

The woman struggles to open her eyes.

"Are you OK?"

She remains silent, staring at me.

"Are you OK?"

"... Yes."

"Thanks for saving me. My name's Martynas."

"Anastasia. Where's...?"

I point at her legs with my eyes. She sees what's under them and abruptly pulls them in, then sits up.

"Alive?"

"No."

"Did I kill him?"

"No, I did. We have to move. Can I call you Ana? Or Nastya?"

"Ana."

Our descent is slow. I cling to the railing, hopping down the stairs since I can't put any weight on my right foot.

Four floors down, we reach the first of two tunnels. Ours is even deeper underground.

I need to pause and rest.

Anastasia wants to run away from here, too. She asks about the escape plan.

In my current condition, *running* sounds somewhat optimistic.

I have only a concept of a plan—break out of the territory and reach the city, then lay low for a while. Gelendzhik is a fairly large resort located near a spacious bay. It has an airport and several marinas. There are bound to be sailboats there.

Unfortunately, it's twenty kilometers away—almost twice that if we stick to the roads.

"I have an idea."

Anastasia has been to the palace before. She's used the tunnel we're heading to on several occasions—it's the easiest way to get to the beach. Just before the exit, there's a Sports room, stocked with paddleboards, surfboards, water skis, and, most importantly, a pile of diving gear.

The stairs finally come to an end. There's a moving walkway in the tunnel, just like at airports. Unlike regular kings, the russian czar does not go on foot, probably even to take a dump. I hop onto the walkway and almost break into tears of happiness when it starts to move. Anastasia stands beside me, offering her shoulder.

The tunnel is exquisite—its tall walls are adorned with redwood. Repin's *Barge Haulers on the Volga* hangs on the wall. The painting begins to move along the wall, in sync with the walkway. The haulers are towing the walkway—witty as hell. It wouldn't surprise me if this were the original, and the one in Saint Petersburg a copy.

"You're Lithuanian?"

"Yes."

"*Labas*[1]"

She greets me in Lithuanian.

"*Labas.* How did you know?"

"That dead hunk of meat told me."

She switches back to russian.

The Sports room is massive. It features a floor of patterned marble, a wooden table with semicircular legs, and a matching set of armchairs. The walls are decorated with topographic contours of a seafloor.

I'm overwhelmed by a sense of *déjà vu.* It feels like I've been here before.

The choice of equipment would make the best dive shop proud: a selection of suits in all sizes and thicknesses, air tanks, fins, watches, underwater harpoons, knives…

Though the item that delights me the most are the kids-sledge-sized diving scooters. I turn one on—**battery level: 99%.**

We grab the thickest suits—we're planning to spend a long time underwater. I sit down and try to remove the jacket. It's torn, dirty, bloody, and ill-fitting. Ana watches me struggle.

"Wait a sec."

She uses a set of dive shears to cut into the sleeve and helps me undress.

Gripping lightly, she flexes my elbow gently.

"Does it hurt?"

"It does."

"Dislocated."

"I suspected as much."

1 *Labas*—"Hi" in Lithuanian.

She finds a towel, wraps it tightly around her arm to make it thicker, then shoves it into my armpit.

"Relax."

Easy for her to say.

With an abrupt move, she thrusts my arm against my body.

The sound it makes is even more sickening than the pain, but it signals that the shoulder is in place.

"It's going to hurt for quite a while."

"Do all angels know how to do that?"

"I'm a physical therapist."

"Then they sent the one I needed."

"I can't help with the leg at this moment."

Even though my arm is somewhat functional now, getting into the suit is still a struggle. Fitting my swollen ankle is especially challenging. Anastasia retreats into the changing room and comes back out while I'm still only halfway through. The form-fitting neoprene reveals the figure of a… ballerina.

Ana is no stranger to diving. She tried it in Egypt a long time ago, and only once after that—here. A couple of years ago, a captain of the palace guard, attempting to charm her into bed, suggested they go fish spotting together. With nothing better to do, she signed off on the dive but turned down the bed part. After the exploratory tour, Vladimir (another one—seriously, is it so hard to come up with different names?) shed his wetsuit, revealing he'd been wearing nothing underneath, and tried to bear-hug her. She responded with a knee to his balls. Disappointed, the paladin of the oceans wound up a punch but, perhaps remembering Ana's importance to the czar, thought better of it. There were no further diving invites.

Anastasia picks out the masks and fins.

"Just one for me, and look for tanks with the largest capacity."

I wouldn't want to use my injured leg for fin flapping.

I finish dressing. We're going to use twenty-liter tanks. I check the pressure: 230 bar. Normally, this would be the time to come up with the dive plan, but there are too many unknowns. We don't even know the speed of the scooters or how long they will last. The single most important task is to make our way outside the territory. If the batteries deplete, we'll move under our own power, and if we run out of air, we'll head to the shore.

Ana hauls the equipment against the wall.

"Now watch this."

She pushes a button. A 2x2-meter section of the floor sinks slightly and slides open, revealing a perforated metal platform. Beneath it is a shaft several meters deep, with water at the bottom.

"It's an elevator to an underwater tunnel. We can use it for direct access to the sea."

I'm delighted that we won't have to walk out in the open—and that we WON'T HAVE TO *WALK*.

I pick a diver's belt off the wall and stash a knife, a Leatherman multitool, and a torch into its many pockets, then strap on a diving computer watch. I cut off a length of rope, tying one end to the scooter's handle and making a loop on the other to be used as a shoulder strap—the scooter is easier to control with two hands. I select a harpoon gun and grab a couple of spare bolts.

We fasten the weight belts—they'll keep us from floating up.

There's a detailed map of Gelendzhik hanging on the wall, marking all the marinas within the mushroom-shaped bay. I commit it to memory, noting a few potential destinations.

We drink some water and eat a Snickers bar apiece (the shelves here are packed with snacks) while I stash a few into my pockets. After checking the tanks one last time, we help each other put them on. The masks and fins go on last.

"Let's go?"

As we descend, the water is coming up to my ankles, shins, knees, thighs. I feel the burning sensation in my deep wounds and a hundred of the smaller ones I didn't even know existed. The platform stops. I hear the hatch above close. It's fine—the illumination here is excellent.

We're diving through a slightly sloping tunnel. Its two-meter diameter makes it feel spacious. It's obviously man-made but decorated to resemble a natural underwater cave. As we move forward, we come across a web-shaped grate. Anastasia presses what looks like a regular rock, and the barrier pivots open.

It comes back to me. I saw it in the movie *Amphibian Man*[1]. Ichtyandr would swim out to the sea through an opening just like this. The Sports room is furnished to mirror the interior of the protagonist's father's house. A goddamn theme park.

1   *Amphibian Man* is a 1962 soviet science fiction romance film.

The scooter's integrated screen displays speed, depth, duration, and battery status. Since GPS doesn't function underwater, we have to rely on the directional compass. That's sufficient—we need to head directly northwest at 315 degrees. We're moving at 15 kilometers per hour, which is impressive for underwater travel. After putting in some distance from the shore, I signal with a thumbs-up that I'd like to surface.

I don't have a valid reason for it, other than an itch to see the results of the fireworks.

It was worth it. Massive columns of smoke rise from the palace grounds as sirens wail in the distance. A red firefighting helicopter is dousing the blazing palace with water while maneuvering over it. Another hovers near the sea's surface, refilling its water tanks through a suspended hose.

Yet another military helicopter circles the location where the Buyan corvette is supposed to be.

Two life rafts are moving toward the shore.

From down here, I can't assess the extent of the building destruction, but I'm sure the plan has slightly exceeded expectations.

While we're still on the surface, I check our position on my watch. Based on the covered distance and battery status, I guesstimate we should be able to reach Gelendzhik.

The batteries held up, almost. My scooter died with half a kilometer left to the bay's entrance. Anastasia is lighter and… more hydrodynamic. This could make a decent compliment, though I'm not sure if I'd dare to actually say it. Hers still had 9% remaining.

It took us an hour and a half to cover twenty kilometers. Ana's scooter is towing us both for the remaining half kilometer. I still hold on to mine—it might still be needed later.

The mushroom-shaped Gelendzhik bay's mouth-stem is 1.8 km wide, the cap—nearly 5 km. The city center and beaches are located on its eastern side, with the airport and seaport to the west. The central docks—long open piers—are not meant for prolonged mooring. On the eastern side, just inside the bay's entrance, is a small closed marina with nearby ship repair shops and storage facilities. We're heading there.

It's getting dark. We round a pier and enter the port through its northern gate. I've got only six bars of air left, Ana—twenty[1]. What kind of compliment would suit *this* situation?

You make me breathless

or

You take my breath away

I survey the hulls of the lined-up vessels. Half of them are motorboats, the rest are sailboats, easily distinguishable by their long keels.

I signal Ana to wait under a motorboat at the end of the pier while I dive to search for a temporary home. The second vessel down the line is another small motorboat, followed by three sailboats, all 10–13 meters long—exactly what I was looking for. The crystal-clear water allows me to see the empty pier. The sun has just set, clearing it of roamers.

I choose the one in the middle—covered in the most bird droppings—suggesting an owner who doesn't spend most of their time

----

1 2.5% and 8.6% of the initial capacity.

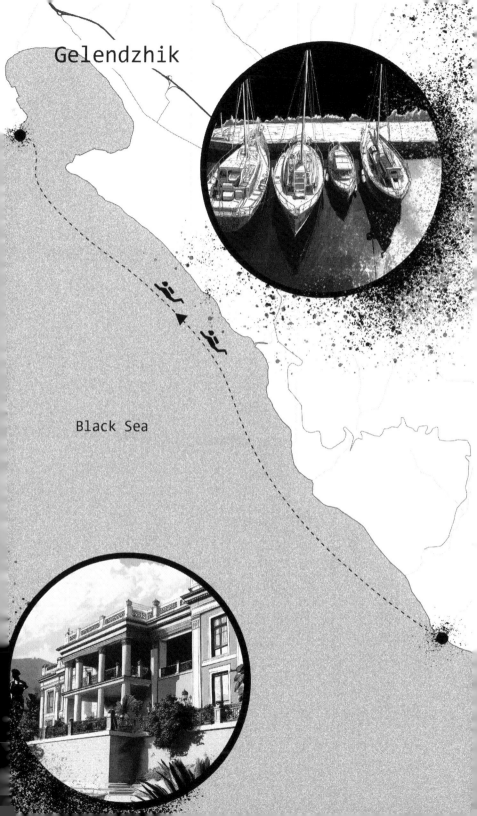

Gelendzhik

Black Sea

on the vessel, cleaning its deck. Nostalgia might've played a role too—it says N390 on its side, a Swedish Najad sailboat, especially prized by long-voyage enthusiasts. When I was younger, I crossed the Pacific in an N441, which is five feet longer.

I gesture for Ana to get closer.

The boat is moored to the pier by its bow. We dive to the stern instead. I surface, push myself up against the swim platform, and grab a small ladder, lowering it into the water. Then, I tie the air tank and the scooter to it.

Puskai! says the red letters on the boat's tail. I like the name—*Let it be!* I'm hoping it lets us be its guests.

People who sail know that most owners leave the cabin keys somewhere on the boat. More often than not, they're kept in a locker accessible from the cockpit. Boats often have multiple owners with just one key, and they are rarely targeted by thieves. I'm hoping this tradition holds even in russia. Worst-case scenario, I can break the lock with the tools I have.

I find the key in the most predictable spot: a cabinet beneath the engine ignition block.

I unlock the wooden door and push the hatch open. Returning to the swim platform, I submerge my hand with a thumbs-up, signaling it's safe to come up. Ana's head breaks the surface. She slips out of the tank harness and hangs it next to mine.

"Pass me the scooters."

I toss them into the cockpit and help Ana climb up. Together, we slip inside the cabin and close the door behind us.

My sole desire is to stretch out, drift off, and sleep—preferably until morning, then through the night, and into the next morning again.

We need to shed the soggy wetsuits. Ana is rummaging through the cabinets and it looks like we've hit the jackpot—they're stocked with clothes and food supplies.

We undo the zippers on each other's backs and undress. It's only been two hours since we met, a significant portion of which was spent underwater in silence, but the nakedness doesn't seem strange—almost.

The clothes we found are at least three sizes too big—both for Ana and me.

"We'd fit right in at a boomer rave dance party."

Ana seems pretty lively.

Police sirens are echoing ceaselessly—distant for now—coming from Gelendzhik center across the bay. They're looking for us. I know they'll come searching here too, sooner or later.

There's a row of small windows in Najad's hull. Two rear ones on the right side—where the master bedroom is located—offer a clear view of the pier's entrance. That's where police or spetsnaz[1] would emerge from. We'd have a minute or so to silently slip into the water.

If we have to flee, we'll need the wetsuits, but there won't be time to put them on. I stuff the fins inside the suits and hang them on the ladder next to the tanks, then return carrying the scooters. Instead of walking, I crawl to avoid having to step on my foot.

A cable runs from the boat to a water and power connection box on the pier. 220 volts are a long-forgotten luxury, but I only have two devices to charge.

----

1   A street term for russian special forces units.

After making sure all the curtains are drawn, I turn on a small light next to the navigation console.

I remove the scooter's batteries. 12 volts—very good. The charging port is proprietary, though—not so good. I find a car power connector, cut the cable at the other end, strip the wires, and twist them directly onto the contacts, wrapping them with insulating tape. It would seem like an easy job if I had all ten fingers. Since I have only five, it takes much longer than it should. A charging indicator lights up when I turn it on.

Ana has the contents of a first aid kit spread out on the bed. She hands me four (!) ibuprofen tablets and a glass of water.

"Give me your foot."

She wraps my ankle with an elastic bandage.

"Get some sleep. I'll take the first shift."

She sits on the bed next to the observation window and unwraps a Snickers bar. I lie down beside her.

"Wake me up in a couple of hours. If you notice anything, just kick me."

I'm out cold in half a second.

[83]

Sleeping through exhaustion is a bit weird. The boat swaying softly, the halyards rapping on the mast, small waves beating against the hull, nothing is letting the subconsciousness go. I know I'm asleep, but somehow, I'm also convinced that I'm not. I can see Ana looking out the window, but I need to make sure. *All good?*—I ask. *Yes*—she confirms, but after just a moment she turns to me—*someone's coming! A man!* I stay lying down, telling her it doesn't matter, he's alone and can't hurt us, we're safe. The man is already aboard, descending the steps to the cabin. It's Professor Pavlov. He has a robotic left hand—just like mine with its skin stripped. *You're dead, I killed you myself*—I say. Professor lets out a psycho's laugh as he looks at his fake hand: *it's perfect!* The perfection grabs him by the neck and starts to choke him, but after a few seconds, it lets go. Professor bursts with laughter again—*Ha ha ha! Did I scare you?!? It was just a joke!*

I snap upright, drenched in sweat.

"How long was I out?"

"A minute shy of two hours."

"Did I speak in my sleep?"

"Nope. You didn't even snore."

I have a lot of work to do. It should've been taken care of before going to sleep, but I was dead tired. Getting out of bed, I realize I can now put weight on my foot—ibuprofen and the bandages helped.

It's Ana's turn to go to bed. We agree to take turns sleeping for four hours—a common duration for a watch on a ship.

Scooter is now fully charged. I connect the other one. The second attempt takes significantly less time—my one-handed skills are coming back to me. I search through the cabinets in the cockpit, looking for an anchor. After tying the wetsuits and air tanks into a bundle, I attach them to the anchor, lower it to the bottom, and secure the rope to the ladder.

I could really use an internet connection, but my robot hand is done for. I sank what was left of it immediately after putting some distance from the palace.

I turn on the VHF radio. It has two pre-set channels: 16, used for security announcements or hailing for assistance, and 73. I leave both as they are and power up the navigation plotter. Both the VHF and the plotter are modern B&G devices, considerably newer than the thirty-plus-year-old sailboat. This particular model has been out of production for a long time.

As the plotter boots up, it displays a map with our location marked on it. A few other small boats with their AIS[1] activated are visible. This system continuously transmits its position via VHF, satellite uplink, or internet, preventing collisions. For years now, all vessels larger than a rowboat have been equipped with it.

I tap our marker, and a table with additional info pops up:

AIS ID: 277199830

It means that AIS is set up on our sailboat, too.

Every half minute, regardless of what I might be doing, I go to the

....

1   Automatic Identification System.

window to check for uninvited guests.

"Sailboat Elbrus is calling Gelendzhik-3."

A transmission comes over channel 73.

"Sailboat Elbrus, this is Gelendzhik-3 listening."

"Five russian citizens entering the bay. We will dock by the White Bride."

"Where are you coming from?"

"Sochi."

"Sailboat Elbrus, proceed to the border control pier for inspection."

"This is Sailboat Elbrus, acknowledged. Heading to border control."

On the plotter, I watch a small boat enter the mouth of the bay. A tap reveals it's a motorboat, moving at a speed of 17 knots. White Bride is a pier in the center of the city, but the motorboat heads in my direction instead. It moves deeper into the bay and docks a bit further from a large industrial harbor. Now I know where the border control office is. I also know that all incoming ships must announce their arrival and are subject to inspection. Let's wait for one to depart.

I inventory the contents of the cabinets: buckwheat, pasta, canned meat, coffee, tea, Alenka chocolate, and vodka (five bottles!). By my count, this should keep two people well-fed for five days. If the food runs out, we can switch to vodka—it has more calories than oil.

Another vessel—a fishing boat—comes in. Off you go to border control. Next up is a transport ship from Azov. They let it pass without inspection.

After two hours, I disconnect the charged battery and lower the scooter to its companion by the anchor.

Halfway through the fourth hour, I run out of things to do, except for surveillance. My eyelids grow heavy.

Flashing blue lights make my eyes snap open, chasing away the sleep. A police UAZik[1] has pulled directly onto the pier, its lights strobing silently.

I'm shaking Ana awake.

A lone figure exits the vehicle, switches on a torch, and heads toward the first motorboat, climbing aboard. I can't see what he's doing, only the dancing beam of light. It takes him a minute at most. We still have eight vessels between us.

Whispering, I reassure Ana that there's no point in diving for an inspection like this. Locking the doors, I turn off the lights and other equipment, then check that the skylights don't reveal any signs of activity inside. After arming Ana with a harpoon, I ready my knife.

After a few minutes, the boat gently rocks once. For those inside the cabin, someone walking on the deck sounds like a running elephant. The policeman is clearly not eager to do his job—he flails his torch sloppily at the windows and rattles the door.

He climbs out of the cockpit, trips on something, and loudly blurts out what he thinks of his night work and his partner back in the car. It doesn't sound like he's fond of either.

He doesn't even board the rest of the boats—after giving them a quick sweep with the light, he heads back.

"Scared?"

"Not really. I know how they work. I doubt that's the end of it, though—there will be others, more competent."

UAZik leaves. I wait ten minutes before instructing Ana to write down all the VHF communications word-for-word and then head to bed.

....

1   UAZ is a russian SUV brand. Their vehicles are universally called UAZiks.

I'm feeling moderately refreshed. After swallowing two more ibuprofen tablets, I dig into the breakfast Ana had prepared. I warned her not to use the gas stove—a drone or helicopter equipped with a thermal camera could've detected that sailboat *Puskai!* was slightly warmer than the rest. We keep the side windows slightly ajar, as even our body heat can raise the vessel's temperature. The breakfast menu consists of buckwheat soaked in cold water, canned meat, and the grim story of Ana's life.

An 08:00 news broadcast interrupts her story—we kept the radio playing in the background. I turn up the volume, and we stop to listen. The russians are claiming that a software glitch caused the launch of anti-air missiles, which did minor (yes, that's how they put it) damage to Alexander Ponomorenko's villa (officially, he's the owner). They'd be closer to the truth if they claimed it was caused by a reckless smoker. Not a single word about the sunken warship.

After breakfast, we clean up, making sure nothing points to us having been here. The reduced stock of buckwheat and cans is hard to hide, though.

I tinker with the VHF, exiting the marine frequencies and leaving only channel 73 open. I experiment with replacing channel 16 with others, finding frequencies used by taxi drivers (who still rely on radios here), truckers, and police. It seems the chaos is affecting everyone—there's a lot of swearing. People are collectively calling the situation *all this bullshit* and asking *when is this going to fucking end?*

Ana heads to bed. I review the notes she took: two transport ships arrived, bypassing border control. Three fishing boats departed— all were inspected.

The sounds of sirens still drift in from the city. Helicopters are constantly zooming around. The airport is nearby, but I doubt its regular traffic is as intensive.

The marina is buzzing during the day. No boats are leaving, but people are in several of them, cheerfully shouting to each other.

"Misha, you have a new one again! I'm telling everything to Irochka!"

A drunken voice yells from a motorboat.

"Go ahead, then watch your boat turn into a submarine!"

Misha is cracking up on his way to the sailboat, a peroxide blonde in tow.

I use the plotter to check the situation at sea near the palace. Two warships have appeared, most likely from Novorossiysk.

Ana is up before noon. We have lunch at twelve—just like regular people. Buckwheat! Canned food! This time, it's my story.

The ships come and go, while the procedure remains the same, except the number of those leaving the bay is growing—presumably due to *all this bullshit*. The border control pier is jammed with boats waiting for inspection. A motorboat departs from our marina, initiates communication, and is directed there as well.

"Sasha, it's me!"

Says a voice from the boat named Koral.

"Sorry, orders."

I write down: Sasha.

At 17:55, Ana suddenly turns to me, her eyes wide.

"Spetsnaz."

I power down all the devices. We put on our masks and step outside to the cockpit. Lying prone on the floor, I replace the door, pull the hatch closed, lock it, and hang the key back in its place. Ana climbs over the left side and, holding onto the railing, silently lowers herself into the water. I do the same. We stick to the scenario we agreed on—diving along the belly of the boat to its stern, where the anchor is tied. Ana, pulling on the rope, descends all the way to the bottom. I untie the rope and follow her. Biting down on our mouthpieces, we turn the tank valves open. If we just sit there, they'll notice the bubbles from our exhaled air. The plan is to exit through the harbor gate, move a couple of hundred meters away, and wait it out. My tank is almost empty, but Ana's should last a while, even if we share it. If hers runs out too, we'll stay on the surface.

I power up the scooter and… turn it off again immediately.

The black bottom of a motorboat hastily approaches the harbor gate, stopping smack in the middle. The escape plan has failed.

Shit.

I look around, searching for the darkest spot in the harbor. At its far end, right next to the spetsnaz SUVs, an old fishing boat is docked. As we dive toward it, we stay to the side, beneath the sailboats and motorboats. Clutching the rope, I tow our wetsuits (yes, we're still wearing our underwater rave party attire). If the spetsnaz come across any signs of us having been there, they'll find us too, even if we turn into goldfish.

As we get under the ship, I check the remaining air—Ana will have to start sharing hers soon. No, we won't have to take turns—every diving setup has an extra mouthpiece.

At the harbor gate, where the spetsnaz motorboat had cut off our retreat, I see dark shapes plunging into the water, enveloped in clouds of air bubbles.

Divers. Shit. Shit.

We press flat against the broad, V-shaped hull between the pier and the ship, hoping the vessel's body will conceal us. The pier is high here, with enormous tractor tires hanging from it to protect the ship's sides. A wind blows from the direction of the gate, keeping the boat firmly pinned. I pop my head up above the surface between two tires. Unhooking the tank harness, I let it hang on a single strap, then put my back against the hull. Finding a good leverage point on the pier's wall with my good leg, I begin to push. A gap opens up.

It would be tricky to explain what kind of acrobatic maneuvers we had to perform or how long it took, but in the end, we had all of our gear—wetsuits, scooters, and tanks—inside one tire, while Ana and I were huddling in another.

My head is at nine o'clock, Ana's just below three. Our knees meet at six. The breadth of the tire is barely enough to accommodate me, with my shoulders firmly squeezed by its sides. Ana has a bit more space. The ship covers us with its hull. There's a porthole on its side, its glass completely matte from countless scratches, letting in a sliver of light.

Water has pooled into a fairly deep puddle at the bottom of the tire, with our wet clothes contributing to it. Both our asses and feet are soaking in it. I use my knife to drill a hole and drain the water. It's marginally better, but our clothes are still wet.

Half an hour passes. It's cold, and Ana begins to shiver. Through our knees pressed together, she infects me too. We adjust the clock.

Now both of us have our feet at around four o'clock. Ana's head is slightly below mine nine.

It instantly gets much warmer.

Another half hour passes. For a while now, my back and locked knees have been complaining about being stuck in this semicircular position and craving a change.

"Do physical therapists have bad backs, too?"

"Ex-ballerinas do."

We hear footsteps and voices drawing closer. Are they heading back to their cars?

Four doors slam shut—one SUV is complete. More footsteps follow. There's a thud, then another. No third or fourth though.

Kicks land on the tire.

I can feel Ana's heart pounding violently.

"Did they check the tires?"

A muffled voice wafts in from outside.

"Dunno."

"Let's check."

Spetsnaz left.

They checked the tires by shooting at them.

I felt the bullets pierce Ana's body.

I don't know how much time I have.

How do I get out of this tire and pull Ana out?

The porthole is made of glass.

Its diameter matches the hip breadth of a certain ex-ballerina.

The Leatherman has a glass breaker.

I lift and bend Ana at the waist to gain some freedom of movement.

The glass shatters on the first hit.

I knock out the remaining sharp shards.

Poking my head in, I see a cabin with a bed directly beneath the porthole.

I push Ana through the hole, feet first.

"I'll be right back."

I let her slip down.

The blood—so much of it—feels warm against my palm.

I push the ship away with my shoulder, then grab onto the railing. Using the tire's rough protector as a ladder, I climb up, lean over the side, and plop onto the deck.

The evening darkness has already set in, but the city lights illuminate my way to the interior door.

It's not locked. I descend and find Ana.

We're back at the sailboat. I carried Ana along the pier. There was no one around, and I didn't have a plan for what to do if I ran into someone. The door is broken, and the inside is an utter mess.

I lay Ana down and cut off her clothes. On the right side of her stomach, near the belly button, is a wound. Another is on her right thigh.

The thick tire absorbed a fraction of the bullets' energy, causing them to lodge in Ana's body. Otherwise, they'd be inside me now. No, I'm not attempting to extract them—that's one of the stupidest ideas, drilled into us by superhero movies. Unless you're a surgeon with the proper tools, you'll only deepen the wound and spread bacteria.

First things first—stop the bleeding. I can dress the stomach wound later since the bleeding isn't very intense. We can only hope no internal organs were damaged.

The wound on the thigh is gushing blood, indicating a damaged artery. Thankfully, it hasn't been severed, or Ana would've bled to death by now. There was a tourniquet in the first aid kit, which I now find flung into the corner. Pleading to angels for it not to be cheap crap, I tighten the tourniquet above the wound. It holds.

"It hurts."

"It has to."

The stream of blood fades away.

I use a cotton wad soaked in vodka to clean the blood from the stomach, then cover the puncture with a few gauze pads and secure them with medical tape.

A tourniquet is safe to keep on for only up to two hours. We now have a couple of options: seek help at a hospital or remove it after applying a makeshift tamponade to the wound.

"I'd rather die."

Ana rejects the hospital option.

I clean the wound and unpack the bandages: one regular and another that has *hemorrhage control* written on it.

"It'll hurt again."

"Give me some of…"

Ana points to the bottle of vodka with her gaze.

I slightly lift her head and bring the bottle to her lips. Frowning, she swallows a few sips.

"Do it."

It's midnight. Ana's asleep. I gave her the last two ibuprofen tablets. She's covered with two blankets, the gas stove cranked up to full blast. After losing blood, she's at risk of hypothermia.

I went out and inspected five sailboats, searching for antibiotics. All their locks had been broken, making my task easier. I came across a sheet of streptocid[1], along with some ibuprofen and paracetamol.

I wake Ana up. Her eyes open, but I can see she's staring off into the distance. I make her swallow both streptocid tablets.

I tune the VHF radio to the border control channel and lie down beside her.

It's raining. Raindrops tap against the hull, washing the blood off the pier and our boat.

---

1   russian antibiotics.

[90]

"Sailboat *Puskai* calling Gelendzhik-3."

"Sailboat *Puskai*, Gelendzhik-3 listening."

"Two russian citizens sailing to Sochi."

"Tolik?"

"Yes, Sasha."

"Say *hi* to Lenka for me!"

"Will surely do."

We spent another two and a half days in the harbor. Assuming lunch breaks were sacred rituals for the border control officers, we undocked precisely at noon. Their eagerness had dwindled long ago—only about one in ten outgoing and one in five incoming vessels were being called in for inspection. The russians weren't following communication protocols, instead holding friendly chats over the radio. From those casual conversations, I now knew the name of the officer on duty.

Following the rules, we notified border control as we set sail. Based on previous chats with dispatch, Tolik—the owner of our boat—knew Sasha. Holding the mic at a distance, I crumpled the foil from an Alenka chocolate wrapper, imitating static in an attempt to alter my voice and disguise my Baltic accent. I didn't ask to pass on regards to Sasha's wife, as I wasn't sure if he had one.

We had no plans to go to Sochi.

Ana didn't look good.

We motor outside the bay. The diesel tank is half full—not enough to cross the sea—but that's what the sails are for. We deploy them after gaining some distance, then head south. Three hours of swaying puts us in international waters—twelve nautical miles from the shore. Crossing this threshold carries symbolic meaning, even if russians would not care, should they catch up with us. The southeastern wind blowing along the shore rules out going straight to Sochi under sail power, making our move away from the land seem like a perfectly legitimate maneuver, in case someone is tracking us and trying to match our course with the declared destination.

We have two options: Georgia or Turkey. The latter is closer, and the wind is favorable. I'm only considering Georgia because the route there would keep us closer to shore. Should Ana's condition worsen significantly, we could seek help ashore. Unfortunately, it would have to be either russia or Abkhazia, which is essentially the same thing.

Ana is burning up, the fever making her delirious. I force her to take the medicine. Once her mind clears, I lay out the options.

"Anywhere but russia."

I switch off the AIS transmitter and adjust our course by 30 degrees, aiming for Samsun, Turkey, 350 kilometers away. If the wind doesn't change and we maintain our current speed of 6-7 knots, we'll be able to say *Selam!*[1] in about 30 hours.

I keep an eye on the plotter. Two warships still patrolling the sea near the palace are joined by a crane ship. They intend to lift the sunken corvette.

Two hours pass, and all the vessels on the plotter disappear. This means we're at least 10-15 nautical miles away from both the shore and the nearest ship from which we can receive AIS data.

....

1   *Hello* in Turkish.

Another twenty nautical miles covered. I make an effort to squeeze in fifteen-minute naps every hour. Under the sprayhood, I set the timer, prop myself against the cabin's wall, and just shut down. At the first beep, I power back on. The first thing I see is our boat's kilwater[1]. I follow it into the distance, hoping there's nothing there. After surveying the horizon through binoculars and checking the plotter, I go to Ana. There's not much I can do for her, except put wet towels on her forehead and talk.

Occasionally, we get close to some transport ship, with markers popping up on the screen. I tap on each one to verify.

After the sun sets, I'll try tuning into non-Russian AM radio frequencies—the waves bounce off the stratosphere and travel a few times farther once it gets dark. Last night, still in Gelendzhik, we learned from a Romanian English-language radio station that satellite snapshots had exposed the true scale of the destruction at the czar's palace, as well as the sunken corvette. The russians have abandoned the software glitch story and switched to blaming Ukrainian hackers. Once in a while, even they get close to telling the truth. They blabbered something about red lines being crossed and threatened an adequate response. Putin remained silent—officially, he's not the owner of the palace.

I hope Z3N3K is lying very low.

....

1   Ship's wake.

I'm deeply concerned about three small ships. Unfortunately, they only *look* small on the plotter's screen. A tap reveals they're russian naval warships. All three departed from Novorossiysk, heading southwest. They adjusted their courses by a few degrees at the point where I switched off the AIS transmitter. The middle one—*Kursant Kirovets*—is now heading in a direction almost identical to ours. AIS indicates that unless we alter our course, we'll pass within 1.2 nautical miles of each other in a few hours.

I wish I could grab a pen and simply cross them off—just like in the paper game, *Battleship*.

I adjust our course and fire up the engine. Our speed increases by two knots, and the distance at the passing point grows, though not as much as I'd like. The AIS transmitter is off, but warships are equipped with powerful radars. Even with only a few metallic parts in our sailboat, they'll almost certainly detect us if they get within a few nautical miles.

We steer toward the darker clouds on the horizon. I hope for a proper storm—waves to obscure the sailboat's hull from radar and rain to reduce direct visibility.

I descend into the cabin. Awakened by the engine's hum, Ana looks at me questioningly.

"They're after us?"

They found us.

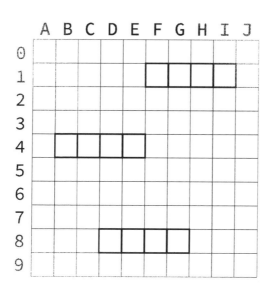

[95]

A powerful beam lights up the sailboat *Puskai!*

The ray is coming from the trailing *Kursant Kirovets*—a Grachonok-class anti-saboteur ship.

"*Kursant Kirovets* calling sailboat *Puskai.*"

Silence.

"Sailboat *Puskai*, *Kursant Kirovets* is calling you."

Silence.

"Sailboat *Puskai*, lower the sails and stop at once."

Silence.

"Sailboat *Puskai*, this is russian warship. We're opening fire."

Shots from a 30 mm cannon ring out as bullets splatter water just a few meters from the sailboat.

"Sailboat *Puskai*, this is the last warning. Stop or we're opening fire at the vessel."

"Russian warship, this is sailboat *Puskai.*"

"Finally. You fucking lost your mind?"

"Russian warship... go fuck yourself[1]."

[96]

The sailboat *Puskai!*, riddled with hundreds of 30mm bullets, sank in the Black Sea at 19:58 on October 6th, 2028.

....
1   A reference to a famous communication between Ukrainian defenders and russian warship: masterversion.net/warship (redirects to Wikipedia)

Dispatch Sasha got off duty at 12:00. Puskai! was the last ship he cleared for exit to the sea. After handing over the shift, he went back home, grabbed a few hours of sleep, and then went out to the city for beers.

At the bar, he ran into his former classmate Tolik.

"Changed your mind?"

"About what?"

"Sochi."

"The fuck you're babbling about?"

"You set sail with Lenka at lunchtime, didn't you?"

They both jumped into a taxi and headed to the harbor. Tolik's sailboat wasn't there. Sasha made the call.

[98]

I release the radio's button and pass the mic back to the captain of a luxury yacht. He doesn't speak russian, but he's familiar with the last phrase—shows me a thumbs-up.

We're speeding towards the Turkish shore. Standing and smiling beside me is... Atari.

"Translate for me?"

Medics down in the cabin are taking care of Ana.

Everything seems to be too good to be true.

But it is.

[99]

A few hours ago. The Black Sea, near Turkish border

When Atari told Eaton where Master was being held, he assumed the role of a savior. He loved playing that part on a global scale, but eagerly embraced this one too—feeling the weight of his blunder. Eaton boarded a special ops unit, a naval captain with his entire crew, and a medic team on a plane. They flew to Sinop, a city in northern Turkey, where a 44-meter motor yacht appropriately named *Escape* waited. He was determined to sail right up to the palace, land an SOF unit, infiltrate, and save the world rescue the prisoner.

A problem emerged on their way: the palace was gone.

Eaton controlled two satellite networks: one provided internet coverage worldwide, while the other took photos of the Earth's surface. Every hour, a satellite would capture a snapshot of the same area. The palace grounds did not look good in those photos. The plan to land on a shore infested with every russian agency imaginable and patrolled by warships was scuttled without much deliberation.

They spent a day drifting nearby without crossing into territorial waters. Eventually, despite Atari's objections, Eaton ordered the ship to return to Turkey.

He sat across from Atari, his eyes cast down.

"Maybe I should give putin a call?"

"And? Will you challenge him to a duel? You tried that already."

"No, I..."

Atari suddenly silenced him with a single commanding gesture of her hand. A special signal pinged in her ear, announcing a message from Master.

```
Hi,

I'm alive but offline and can only transmit a limited
amount of information:

554399660/2

See you soon,

Yours, Master
```

After tapping on her phone for a minute, Atari looked up.

"Turn back."

A forward slash—a division symbol.

```
554399660 / 2 = 277199830
```

277199830 was the AIS identifier for *Puskai!* The first Google result linked to a marine traffic page, displaying the boat's location when the vessel's transmitter was switched on.

On a plotter, Atari tracked *Puskai!* as it left Gelendzhik bay and sailed south. The distance to it was 350 kilometers, about a six-hour trip.

After three hours, *Puskai!* disappeared from the plotter. Fortunately, they still had access to Eaton's satellites. By observing hourly snapshots, Atari noticed the sailboat change course and head almost directly toward them.

She also saw the warships closing in.

With an hour to go, *Puskai!* altered its course once again. It didn't appear in the next shot, having slipped under the cloud cover. The captain of *Escape* steered them toward the projected interception point, while the entire crew combed the horizon for a light or a sail.

Just after dark, the three russian warships altered their courses. The maneuver could only mean they had zeroed in on us. Since we wound't show up on their radars yet, I assumed they had located us via satellites. I changed our heading again, taking advantage of the cloud cover. After completing the maneuver, I caught sight of distant navigation lights straight ahead.

I checked the plotter—empty.

Could anything be worse than three warships pursuing us?

Doubtful.

I lit an emergency flare.

[EPILOGUE]

The sailboat *Puskai!* continued its journey alone on autopilot until its hull was riddled with holes and it sank.

How did I relay my message to Atari?

Heading into the gray zone, I know that the connection is not guaranteed. My robot hand might run out of power, or it could simply be taken from me.

I've come up with several ways to relay a message about myself.

Before leaving Gelendzhik, I broadcasted the following message over the radio channels used by truckers and taxi drivers:

```
           The first 10 to visit
          iphone20.me/554399660/2/
             win the new iPhone!
```

Most figured it out as some kind of scam, but a few took the bait. One was enough.

The sucker typed in the address, triggering a script that sent the message to Atari.

I've prepared a few different domain names for situations like this. One messages Atari, another contacts the commander of the streamer legion. There's also one that sends a note to my mom...

Everything after the / is transmitted as the information I want to pass on. I could've sent anything—coordinates or text like *iloveyou*. Instead, I sent a lightly encoded AIS ID number for *Puskai!*.

What would I have done if there hadn't been a radio lying around, you ask?

I'd send a message in a bottle.

Pub Špunka is packed. With difficulty, shielding my still hurting ribs, I trudge toward the counter.

"Four IPAs."

Atari, Ana, and Z3N3K didn't even try to get inside—they wait sitting beneath the wings of the Angel of Užupis[1]. You could say it's almost hot in Vilnius today—the best day of Indian summer.

It's the first time I'm meeting Z3N3K in person. He's more of a local here than I am, having lived in Vilnius for a long time. I always thought he was younger, but it turns out we're about the same age.

"Будьмо![2]"

He raises his glass, eyes riveted on Ana—or rather, his eye, as his right one is covered by a pirate's patch. He was injured during the first year of the war and switched to hacking.

"Будьмо!"

We echo.

I'm holding the glass in my left hand. It's V 2.0 beta. Just above the barely visible connection is a fresh tattoo:

....

1 Užupis is an artsy district in Vilnius. Its centerpiece is a statue of an angel, known as Angel of Užupis: masterversion.me/angel (redirects to Wikipedia)

2 Budmo!—Cheers! in Ukrainian.

[AFTERWORD]

Master Version 1.1 is my first book. A big thank you to everyone who helped write it. I won't list names—you know who you are.

I've been writing for most of my life—not books, but code. I'm a software programmer. Together with Martynas Majeris, who translated Master Version 1.1 into English, we run a tiny company—essentially a two-and-a-half-man operation (sans Charlie)—but one that's extremely successful in its field: amCharts.com. We estimate that our data visualization libraries are now used by at least half of the Fortune 500 companies and thousands of smaller businesses.

Besides this main activity—which, even after nearly two decades, is still fun—I also enjoy long-distance bike travel and participate in competitive sailing events, both fully crewed and double-handed.

When it comes to my reading habits, I prefer science fiction. Like most readers, I have my favorite writers, such as Neal Stephenson, and eagerly await their new releases. In between, I enjoy giving new authors a try. Sometimes, they blow me away and become new favorites, like Andy Weir. Unfortunately, there's also a fair share of disappointment.

Every time I felt let down by a new book, I thought, I could do better. On one such occasion, I sat down and wrote my first chapter. Then I wrote another. And a couple more. When I tentatively showed them to Martynas, his verdict was along the lines of: *Hm, this shit is actually quite good.* Encouraged, I continued writing, with Martynas offering advice along the way.

To make my texts believable, I wrote about things I know well. As a member of the Lithuanian Riflemen Union—an organization of voluntary fighters ready to take up arms and fight russians if they come this way—and a regular participant in tactical drills and exercises, I'm well-versed in warfare. I know my way around guns and drone combat. During his brief visits home, my close friend Arūnas Kumpis, who has been fighting on actual battle-fields in Ukraine—mostly with drones—since the beginning of the full-scale war, has been keeping me updated on the situation there and how quickly things change.

After finishing the book, I showed it to professional critics, who encouraged me to have it published. The first edition—written in Lithuanian—hit bookshelves in November 2024. Since Lithuania's population of 3 million doesn't provide a huge sci-fi fanbase, I decided to translate Master Version 1.1 into English and try my luck internationally. Somehow, I managed to persuade Martynas, who isn't a professional translator, to take on the job. I knew his English was good enough, but the result still surprised me.

Lithuanian is quite unique and very different from English, belonging to a distinct language branch shared only with Latvian. By the way, never make the mistake of asking a Lithuanian if their language is similar to russian—that's an insult. It's not even remotely similar, as it's not a Slavic language. Martynas found a way to make the text sound good in English, which was no easy task. Many verbal expressions, locations, situations, and references had to be adapted to be comprehensible to an international audience (see Translation Notes). Honestly, I believe the English version of the book turned out even better than the original.

I hope you enjoyed reading it! If you did, please consider leaving your feedback on **Goodreads** and **Amazon**, and recommending it to your friends. Let's make this book Lithuania's first international bestseller. And don't forget to support Ukraine's fight for freedom by donating to relevant causes. Thank you!

Send your feedback to the author: `am@masterversion.net`

[TRANSLATION NOTES]

The names

Some names—especially aliases—were modified from the original to enhance fluency and readability. As an example, Zenek originally went by his "hacker name" 3EHEK. In cyrillic-based languages like Ukrainian, "3" looks like the letter "Z", and "H" is read as "N". However, for anyone not familiar with the cyrillic alphabet this would make an awkward read. Since Zenek is a prominent character, I took the liberty of replacing it with Z3N3K. It still carries the cheesy shallowness of the "l33t" name-making but reads without breaking one's mental tongue.

The terms

There's a fair share of local slang terms in the book, too. I foraged the web trying to find the closest matches in English for those. For example, a widely used term "morozas" means a rough, slightly dumb brute, dressed in some predictable way (e.g. training suit), acting all macho. But I can't add all that shebang in the book, so I went with a "thug".

The geographical names

We also made a decision to omit some geographical names. Most people might know Vilnius (if you don't, look this gem of a city up right now) but names like "Antakalnis" likely won't ring any bells for anyone not living in Lithuania. I replaced it with a "quiet Vilnius neighborhood" so the reader can experience the same sentiment of the moment by applying whatever feelings or references the "quiet neighborhood" evokes to them personally.

The regional specifics

Sometimes a brand is used so often, it is elevated to a generic term. Then we go and google stuff or photoshop our profile pictures. Some of those are regional. For instance, in this nook of the world, any crystal-based decoration is likely to be referred to as "swarovskis" (Swarovski is a brand producing crystal jewelry), but might raise eyebrows anywhere else. We came to a decision to replace such non-universal genericides with generic names, like "crystal-studded".

The use of russian words

In the original, some of the labels are written in russian language. While they contribute to the authenticity of the specific situation, we decided to replace the cyrillic words with their Latin transliterations for easier reading, instead of providing them in the annoying footnotes. Only a few non-essential places were left as in the original, because the mood was just right.

The units of measure

The book is full of technical details and therefore permeated with measurements that use the metric system. We tried to provide imperial equivalents in footnotes, but that cluttered up the text, so we decided against it.

The military time

"Military time" is used throughout the book, as the 12-hour style would contrast with the general premise of a warzone.

[SYNOPSIS]

Master is a lone soldier, relying on near-future technology and his own creativity to survive in the Gray Zone of the Ukrainian warzone.

The year is 2028. The simmering conflict has transformed into a new kind of battlefield, where military streamers compete for followers and views while carrying out often deadly missions.

Armed with an arsenal of experimental technology—including an advanced computer-brain interface, a multifunctional prosthetic arm, AI, and drones controlled with his mind—Master embarks on a desperate run for his life as he searches for missing fellow streamers.

www.masterversion.net

Printed in Poland
by Amazon Fulfillment
Poland Sp. z o.o., Wrocław

45848401R00131